BEYOND RUST

For Jose

Larry Smith

*Who knows and cares
and tells the stories –*

Larry Smith

Working Dogs Series
Bottom Dog Press
Huron, Ohio

Cover photography
by Charles Cassady, Jr.

Acknowledgements

The author would like to acknowledge the following publications, in which some of these stories first appeared.

Canto and *New Waves* for portions of *Beyond Rust: A Novella*
The Heartlands Today and *Ohio Magazine* for two versions of "Bingo at the Mingo Show."
The Plough: North Coast Review for "To The Landfill."
The Heartlands Today and *In Buckeye Country: Photos and Essays of Ohio Life* for "The Company of Widows."
Mark: A Journal of Scholarship, Opinion, and Literature: for "Home Casualties," "Inside the Smoke," "Outside the Millgate," "Climbing the Mountain."
Liars' Corner Almanac for "Woman Voices."

I want to thank my wife Ann and my family for their advice and continued support. And to the members of the Firelands Writing Center, I extend my thanks.

****** CONTENTS ******

BEYOND RUST

A Novella

"Different things were important, and we understood
the same things differently, often markedly differently.
It is often difficult to figure out what's going on
around you even when you're not blindfolded."
                                        -Terry Anderson (*Den of Lions*)

Special thanks to those who assisted with the research
for this novella: Bill Wright, Michael E. Waldecki, and
to Auggie and Mary Waldron who opened their home
and their records of the Lorain lockout to me. It is a
work of fiction based on the real struggles of working
people. The actions of UAW leaders Al Pena and
Frank Valenta to save the Union and the mills are a
matter of public record.

THE BIG WAIT

I sit here outside St. Mary's Catholic Church on Reid Avenue in downtown Lorain, knowing that my car won't start. I walked over here this morning down Elyria Avenue to where it meets Broadway at the Journal Building, then over to Reid—a long walk in the dusty morning air for anyone. I abandoned my car here last night, and about an hour ago I passed any hope of its ever starting, so I am waiting now for a lift from my girlfriend Maria, if she can get off work.

An old man in a nice blue coat is picking up trash around the apartment building on 7th Street where it dead ends. So many streets dead end in my neighborhood, cut off before they can go anywhere.

This old man is sitting on the bench now having his second cigarette of the day as a schoolbus full of kids slides down Reid Avenue. I light one up too and take a long drag as the car fills with smoke like old Lorain when the mills were running and everyone had jobs. Now what we have are the bars on Broadway and our coffee and our cigarettes. I am thinking of getting me something at Avanti's Bakery on the corner, only I don't want to miss Maria who could come to rescue me from my car at any moment, or not.

This is when I begin writing all this down, like it's something to do with my head and hands, take out my 79 cent Bic Pen, and on the back of my old inventory sheets, start taking down what I see and think.

I am looking up at the street when I notice the shadow of someone beside me at the window, which I have just cracked for the smoke. It's that old man in the blue jacket, and he's talking, so I roll the window down.

"...Something...wrong with your car, Buddy? Do you...want any help?"

He has this pause in his speech so that I know he is retarded, and his eyes are big like he's excited about finding me here. This guy is pretty old for being a retarded person out on the streets in a new blue jacket.

"Thanks, no," I say, shaking my head. "The car is dead," and I motion with my hands like I'm signaling safe at home, only my fingers splayed. He understands and nods. "I'm waiting for a ride to work." And we both nod.

"It's okay," he says towards my face, and I notice how really nice he is dressed with a clean buttoned shirt and well groomed hair. His eyes are soft and generous, and I am thinking he is taking a big chance out on these streets evening or morning, because a lot of drugs do go down right here in the parking lot, or so I hear.

Maria hasn't shown, so I decide to ask this old man to get us both a coffee up at the Avanti's on Eighth Street. He takes my two bucks and says "Sure. I'll be right back." He repeats "right back" four times I think. I watch him walk away and I'm thinking how I may be giving my money away.

As I watch him cross at the corner and head south, I write all this down. It passes the time, till I catch this young Puerto Rican girl jump out of her boyfriend's car and walk toward the building. She is walking fierce like she and her man just had some wicked fight and she's shaking her little tail feathers back in his face. She is wearing one of those white uniforms for cleaning, only real short, and my heart starts thumping in my throat, you know, like you can't swallow it, and she is so pretty, her brown skin next to the white. She looks right at me, and I give her the nod, "Give it to him, sister."

She laughs and smiles pretty while turning into her building to a day of cleaning and listening to the old people inside. I bet she gives them the story of her fight with Juan as she's turning the doilies on their old couches and chairs. And she'll say how a white guy in an old beatup Buick waved her on. See, I'll be part of her story as she is part of mine.

I look up just now and the old man is standing at the corner looking around. In his hands are our coffees, but he looks lost. His memory wasn't long enough.

So I open the car door and walk towards him. At first he doesn't know me, is surprised maybe at my cane and begins to turn away.

"It's okay, old man," I say, "I'm the one from the car." And he stops shaking and holds out my cup. "Thanks, amigo," I hear myself say. "Muchas gracias," comes out of my lips. I even shake his hand, and his face smiles back as the sun rises over the black silhouette of the mill. Around the corner come the wild cries of the children from playground at St. Mary's School. I look down and notice how my cup is empty, but it doesn't matter anymore, really. This old man is as happy as I am to be standing together here in the warm August sun with its forgiveness and promise.

By the time I finish writing this, Maria has pulled up and is revving her engine and giving me the eye.

Ave, Maria, you rescue me.

THE JOB

"Tomorrow," she says and walks away, shaking her big butt in my face.

"What time?" I ask, leaning with my wrists on the counter.

"Six," she says, walking through the kitchen doors. "Sharp!"

"I'll be here," I say, though what I'd like to do is throw my coffee on her cold back. Who does this Cassandra think she is? She went to school with my sister Loretta and lived just around the block. Someone should tell her there ain't no queen of Lorain, Ohio, unless it's for the International Festival, and this one, believe me, is no beauty.

I turn and walk away, save my spit for the street.

How come these little victories—like getting a job, even as a dishwasher at $3 an hour with no benefits—don't taste more sweet? How come? My grandmother, she used to say "The crust is hard, but the bread is good." And what the heck that means, I'm still not sure. Anyway it starts me thinking about her good homemade rolls, and then I stop feeling so mean. The only way to show a woman like that Cassandra is to outwork her image of you, and I've been doing that all my life, even before getting my leg all tore up in the mill. I've been small most of my life, and we've always been poor. But I want nothing for that. Just watch me work. You'll see, Cassandra of the Moloch.

I push my way out the door and walk all the way up to the corner without my cane. Sometimes the pain is comfort. The bus will come in ten minutes and I can be home in half an hour. When Maria comes in from her work all tired, I will kiss her face into a smile. I will bring her some wine while she bathes. I will wash her smooth back, kiss the water from her dark arms and legs ...

I am writing this in my notebook now on the bus, but I am going to quit for a while and dream...

In the apartment now, I write... Today I have a new job at Rudy's Deli and Cafe. Our celebration must be small, for no one can know or I will lose my disability check and we will never be able to buy a used car for me or a computer for Maria. I will work this job so we can do more than pay rent and eat.

For tomorrow and tomorrow and tomorrow's tomorrow I will awaken in the dark, dress while Maria sleeps, then drink my first coffee, write in this notebook, then catch the bus. I will show up at the restaurant early and slip into Rudy's back door before the sun rises. I will wash the pans that have cooked the food and the plates that serve it, making all things clean. I will stay out of the reach of that witch Cassandra, and I will slip back out the door for the 2:00 bus home. I will come home and write again, then put dinner on for me and Maria. This is the rhythm I will work my life around. It is what I have and who I am, and though the taste is plain, it is not without its sweetness.

THE RIDE

On Sunday we go out to the house of Maria's mother, Esther. She is a big beautiful woman with raven black hair and deep brown, animal eyes. She likes me and says I remind her of her brother José, who is a roofer now in Cleveland. I've met José several times at Esther's place, and I can't see the resemblance. He's built like a tree, tall and stalky. So it must be how we both like to use words—José is a talker. He gives speeches all the time on Native American Cultures and Rights, and me, what I have to say, I write.

Anyway we stop at the Midway Mall to pick up a new silk blouse for Esther's birthday. Back on the road I begin playing with Maria's skirt as she drives. It is pretty with flowers and also made of silk. I begin sliding it up her legs a little at a time, gently stroking the warm side of her thigh, when she says, "Marco, you better stop that." It's funny, because the way she says it reminds me of my mother scolding me for something, and thinking of that makes me stop, but I give Maria a good kiss on the neck where her dark hair is pulled back in a short pony tail.

"Do you want to ask my brother about his Ford truck today?"

"No," I sigh. "I don't have the money to even ask. And please, I don't want to tell them about my job."

"Ah, Marco, why not? You know, you can trust my whole family. We're a family of trust, and besides, we've all got something on each other, so nobody dares to talk."

I allow my silence to speak for me.

Maria pulls onto Route 113 heading west, and I watch how well she drives. I love the way this woman moves, so sure and smooth like a cat who has learned to stay alive. I open my window for a while and let the September wind rush over our bodies. It is good to be here with Maria heading to a good meal with family and friends. Let the wind and music take us there. Why do I ask for anything more?

"Marco," Maria begins, and then from nowhere (like she always does), "Do you miss your mother?"

"Sure," I say without needing to think. "What kind of person would I be if I didn't?" but that is not going to end it, I know.

"Yes, yes, I know you were a good son and all that" putting her hand on my good leg. "It's just that sometimes from somewhere inside of you I feel a sadness. Is that what's troubling you?"

She is leaning towards me now as I stare out through the dirty window. I cannot hide anything from this woman. "Maria, I could begin to talk of it but could I stop?"

She waits at the light and sighs, "Why don't you try." Shifting up through the curve, "We have all day."

"Okay, Maria, I'll tell you how it feels. It's like...being an orphan, like being an orphan again and again and again. Losing first my little sister to leukemia, then my father, and then Mom. After my accident and the struggle with drugs, even my brother Ted turned from me. It's like having the mill close and abandoning us all to the will of things—Survive on your own, life seems to call out to me, over and over—Here is this joy, this pain, live with it 'cause it's really all the same."

The wind has become cool, and I try to say it once more, "Maria, you know the old Giant Tiger building over on Elyria Avenue, how it's all so big and empty and closed up and alone...well, sometimes it feels just like that."

And without taking her eyes off the road Maria says this remarkable thing about how they are all still there. "They're still inside of you, Marco. Can't you tell. Only thing is, you just might have to let go of them, so you can have them back again."

The car is whipping past trees and houses as I begin to let out the pain, this wild groan that comes out of my chest. And then Maria stops the car at a green light on Baumhart Road, and the traffic behind us starts honking for us to move on. But no one honks at Maria. She just ignores it and reaches up to my face. "Oh, Baby," she says, "Oh, Baby, you shouldn't be so sad. I'm here for you." She unbuckles and slides up on her seat and swings her leg around straddling me. Then she is kissing me as the cars pull around, and I can feel her beautiful chest breathing against me and the rhythm of her heart beating into mine. Her lips make me forget everything, just everything, and I am pressing her warm back as she rubs her pretty silk dress into me. And together we forget everything, everything but each other there on the road to Mama's, till all I know is I can't love this woman enough.

FIESTA

"It's Maria and Marco!" shouts Juanita, Maria's little sister, as we walk through the family room into the bright kitchen light. All of her family seems to be comfortably squeezed into this big melting pot room, along with the sweet smell of corn tortillas and cooked beef.

"Buenas días!" several shout as Luis strums a loud chord sending Maria into a happy dance around the table. Her eyes flash as she turns, glancing back at me. And the men shout and the women clap as someone hands me a cold bottle of Corona.

I am always glad to be here, where the music of life flows in from the deep eyes to the quick movement of hands and feet. A young cousin is handing me a plate of beans and rice and a huge enchilada.

"Hey, Marco. Dance with me," calls Maria, but I lean on the doorsill and hold up my beer to salute. Before you know it a cousin is dancing along with her, his arm around her waist. Someone is stamping their feet when Luis starts singing.

Why can't the week be full of Sundays like this? Why can't Maria dance her life among the people who love her? And for a moment I look out the back porch door to the September fields where the crushed stalks of corn lie like gold upon the brown earth. This old farm house rises square on the broad field, and it is full of light and warmth. Being here is like taking a bath in music as I close my eyes and feel the room shake with it. When I get home I will write it all down, as much as I can.

"Marco, come, please. Out onto the porch." It is Esther, Maria's mom, tugging on my arm, but gently.

"Sure," I smile back and rise still balancing my plate.

"Let's sit," she sighs pointing to the swing made empty by a swish of her hand. Kids jump down onto the yard. "Sit, Marco, and eat. I want to talk with you."

I have known Esther for a year now—almost as long as Maria—and this is the first time she asks me to talk like this. I take a good forkful of beans and rice and wait for her to speak. The music of the kitchen spills outside the windows. First she begins to swing softly and I am so close I can smell her sweet rose cologne, I can see the sharp lines at the corners of her eyes.

"You are not afraid, Marco, to become part of such a wild family?" It is a statement as question and I must think how to answer.

"No, I'm not afraid," I finally say. "I love being with you here, as I love Maria." Speaking the truth makes all things true.

Esther touches my arm with her hand and I know this is what she waited to hear. Like one who gardens tomatoes and peppers, she has not interfered but merely fed and waited. Like one who does not open the oven door, she has allowed us to bake. I am feeling this in the silence she has allowed.

"Marco, Maria is like a bird, like a bird that loves to fly and sing." I nod. "But a bird that has never nested or stayed inside the yard." She looks me right in the eyes, and I am feeling an extra pulse here in what she says. "Marco, from the day Maria was born on the way to the hospital, I knew her as a child of the wind. Do you understand?"

"Yes, Esther, I think I know."

"I know that you know. But do you understand?"

I shrug my shoulders lightly.

"Well, Marco, when you *realize* what I'm saying about Maria, then you will know what to do. I pray you will find a way to keep Maria tame and yet free. That is all."

We sat there gently swaying for a long time listening to the music and the birds in the yard. And, as I ate her food bite by bite, with each moment the taste grew more.

THE AWAKENING

"Marco! Get up! The alarm didn't work!"
That is how I woke to it, that and Maria rolling out of bed, her little footsteps running across the floor to be first in the bathroom. In my bare feet I pad out into the kitchen still not awake standing at the sink filling the Mr. Coffee—water/ then filter/ then coffee/ turn it on. I step towards the refrigerator and my feet feel it the same time as my nose—"Cat Piss!" I yell at the window and jump to a safe space. "Late....and cat piss to start my day," I say out loud to myself, the way we all do. Still mad I tear off a paper towel and start wiping one foot, balancing on the other when I knock the clean pans onto the floor and turn to face Maria standing there naked in the light, the wet mane of her hair still dripping.
"Jesus, Marco, what is it?" And we both stand and stare as though someone has just snapped our picture, and we can suddenly see ourselves standing there naked and open mouthed. We both start to laugh. I mean real laughing till finally the cat peeps its head out from under the table to see if we are crazy or what, and I chase Maria back into the bathroom—but she is too quick for me—and I go back to see if the coffee is coffee yet. The sun is tweaking the darkness with a nice morning rise and shine, and I know I am late.
Maria drives me to work just for today. She figures she can more risk being late. Anyway she phones Bob at Compu-Graphics to say she has had a little accident. In fifteen minutes tops, we are pushing the cat out the door, starting the Ford Fairlane, and driving down Highland Park to Broadway. I hold her coffee on my lap till we whip into the

parking lot. I leave Maria with a kiss and coffee and walk to the back door of Rudy's Deli at exactly 7:00 am. I am not late. Cassandra is standing there with a broom staring at my face like a witch, and I slip off my jacket. "Here! Do the front around the tables and counter, then back here," and pushing her finger into my chest, "Don't leave nothing behind. We keep this place looking spic and span. You get me, boy?"

"Sure," I say and look up to see the old guy, who I learn is Carlos from Canada, smiling back my way. He makes a funny Italian gesture where he slides his finger tips along up under his chin then fans them out like a feather as he tilts up his head. Sometimes I've seen just a tilting of the head as if to say, "It's all a bullshit. So I'm letting it go." And I do.

I grin and signal Carlos with my thumb up in an "I'm Okay—You're Okay—It's all Okay" gesture. I dance the broom over the tile floor and it all becomes just another way of starting the day.

SCHOOL DAYS

I'm on break now, sitting out in Carlos' car behind the cafe writing this, and I'm remembering long ago when I was fourteen. I went to old Lorain High School just two blocks from here. It wasn't so rough back then. My biggest hassle was in always getting there late. Every week I'd have to sit through detentions. I had to take care of my little sister JoAnn: getting us some kind of breakfast, then waiting for her to catch her bus. That's why I was always late. After school Mom would be home, so it was okay if I came in late. Tell you the truth, I don't think she ever *knew* that I was late. I know she never asked.

Anyway, what I started to write here was about how I started this writing thing back then in detentions. That was my break, really. And while Bear Koba or The Face Gubric were snoring into their leather jackets spread across their desk, and Linda Lips and Sylvia Sconce were passing notes to each other or long looks at Coach Heydinger, I was sitting along the windows writing furiously into my story notebook, a Big Chief, red with that black binding bar taped across the top and that neat drawing of the good chief peacefully in the center. I must have filled fifty of them.

My first stories were about Moon creatures and space explorers, kid stuff really. Then I did a string of ghost stories I used to pass around, and some of the kids liked them a lot. But what they loved most were my gang tales using their own names and features. "A Knife in the Shower" was a sexy one about a fight in the girl's lockerroom. I just watched people and made things up that I thought could happen. I followed the shower story up with a murder mystery set in the school's basement where a white kid kills a black kid for touching his girl and then the teacher turns him in. Most of my friends loved the first part and hated the ending. I learned about audience that way. Today that school's mostly Black and my story might get a better reading. But back then, I swear, I only thought about telling a good story.

I'm remembering how a week ago I was parked on 6th Street at the corner of Lorain High School. I was there to pick up Maria's sister's girl, Angelina. When school let out at about two-thirty, a pack of Black kids came over and sort of leaned on Maria's car. I didn't do a thing when I saw them coming. I just stopped writing in this journal and leaned back in the seat.

"What you want sitting here, Man?" someone called through the windowshield. A girl rubbed her lipstick lips on my window glass. Someone put their loud boombox on my hood. I could wait this out, and though I did nothing to deserve it, I recognized, neither did they. It was just some dumb racial reaction to who we all were, all of us caught in our clothes, our blood and culture, forced unspeakably into the slavery of it. Yes, I could wait this out.

When they started rocking the car, that's when I turned on the engine and slipped her into gear. I didn't want Angelina running out into this. And just then, as things sometimes do in this crazy life, a police car pulled around the corner as Angelina came out the side door, and I pulled over to where she stood.

"I'm sorry, Marco. I really am." And I could see that she meant it. Her soft dark eyes held me to her truth. "It's the way it is here." She was almost crying by then. "I just can't help it."

"It's okay, Angel," I say touching her soft shoulder, and I feel her cool hair as she turns toward the hooting faces of boys in brown jackets and bright caps. "Everything's okay. Really. It's not you, not me, not even them, just something in the air." She keeps looking down at the rubber floormats, so I jam it. "We're out of here," and we pull away toward the town fountain and the old Antler Hotel.

The afternoon light is filling the car now—warm sunlight as we turn along Route 6 toward Lakeview Park with its huge cement basket of flowers when I think to ask, "Angel, why were you late?"

And without looking up, she whispers, "I had a detention. I'm real sorry. I mean it." But I don't care anymore, really, because I can see in her lap that her hands are holding tight to something, and that something is a worn Big Chief notebook.

TALKING IT OUT

Maria says I have to stop wanting everything to end happy. I don't know if she's talking about my life or if she's been reading this notebook..

"Why?" I ask her the next day when we are sitting on the couch watching the Sunday morning news.

"Why what?" she looks over and into my eyes.

"Why should I stop?"

"Marco!" she sighs, then tosses a pillow gently into my face. "Stop what?"

I like seeing her eyes light up like this, like she's angry but happy still. So I tell her, "Stop wanting things to end happily, like you said the other night."

"Ah," she sighs again, "I thought we were done with that." And she takes hold of my hands and says softly, "Marco, it was just a feeling I had."

"But what's wrong with it, really?" I insist. "I mean I tried, Maria, but I just don't get it." And I press the control to "Mute," where everything turns to a ghost pantomime. "Shouldn't we all be trying to make things turn out better, sweeter? I don't get it really. What else are we living for?" Those words just come exploding out of me somehow like a flock of starlings from a bush.

Maria is still looking into my eyes to see if I really mean it, and I do. "Okay, then Marco. What I said to you yesterday was that you have to stop wanting everything to end happy. Because it don't...or doesn't... whatever...and you'd better know that. I watch you, and it's like you want everything to be like in the old movies on that American Classics channel."

"Come on, Maria. What are you saying, that I'm wrong for believing in hope?"

"No, I'm not saying that. What I'm saying is that you have to realize that life just isn't some old musical. Old Life...it keeps on being itself—life. And you, Marco, just end up making yourself sad expecting that it's going to end happy every damn time."

She is really cooking now, and I can see how her skin is getting warm all over. So I take another drink of the iced tea she made after work, and it is clear and cool and sweet.

"I can see what you're saying now," I tell her. "You're telling me how life is *life*, how it is what it is, and that it's all the same."

"Yea, that's it," and I can see that she is almost happy. "Only this too, Marco. That your accepting this is not the same as your giving up or giving in," and she touches my cheek to help me understand. "Honey, I wish you could know this for yourself. Making the world all better than it is might seem a way to protect yourself, but it isn't. Because it closes your heart to the real sadness and joy there. I see you hurting yourself, and it keeps breaking my heart for loving you."

I have to feel my way through the next few minutes, because what she's saying is so close and true. I can't breathe for the pain I'm feeling. It's like waking up and someone is coming toward you and you can't see to think. Maria is crying a little now, and I have to stand up to get it all.

Outside the screen door the sun is turning everything into gold, and I walk through to it. "Maria, come out here with me? Please." And she gets up off the couch and walks out to where I am sitting on the little wooden porch swing that we picked up at a garage sale. We sit there for a long time still and close rocking slowly. Maria is leaning then melting into my arms, and I want to tell her how I love her sitting there with me looking out across our little yard and the alley with its trash cans and old cement block garage, hearing the neighbor's talking in the kitchen and our own little tv still on, and here we are just feeling the air and light.

I want to tell her that I know what she says is true, and that knowing that, I will still keep writing my stories, because life does work out and we do somehow go on. I want to tell Maria all this in the golden light but I just hold her instead, because some things are just too sweet for words.

SOMETHING ELSE

I am thinking about what Maria said last night about opening my heart to the pain, so I decide to write this.
Maria's friends are from South Lorain, mostly. And mine are mostly from the East Side and West Side. It makes no difference, but it does. I mean I used to be afraid to drive through the Subway Park section because I didn't want those Puerto Rican guys to stop me in my dad's car and maybe bang on the hood. They never did, you know, but is that because they just wouldn't have or because I managed to avoid them. We never know these things, and yet we continue to operate under them.

And the thing I'm thinking now is how Maria might have been one of those sweet dark haired girls sitting on the front porch steps watching my car drive by too quickly. Or maybe she was one of those girls in tight cut-off jeans on the swings in the park or in a short flowered dress standing with long flowing hair on the steps of Sacred Heart Church. Maybe she was wondering then what kind of guys drive by so fast, without even looking.

In high school I would be out there to pick up my friend Kenny Farkos over behind the Witier Junior High building. We would probably be picking up some beers and a cup of worms from his Dad's garage refrigerator; then we would take them down to the park by the dump to drink and fish for the carp. We would go back through the trees to a little place that had a big flat rock where we could lay out without our shirts and talk about the women and school and the women.

Kenny would tell me some real exciting stories about his cousins in Southern Ohio, these two country girls who really liked to test out a boy's lips. Kenny was my best friend, and he had this spiked red hair and freckle face. He would tell me stories about Libby and Loretta smoking in the barn and taking off their tops, really driving me mad. But the thing about Kenny was how he could really enjoy my telling a story. He had this really good laugh like a bunkhouse cowboy or something, and he would lie on that flat rock with his belly just shaking with laughs.

He also had this real dark side sometimes when he would look up at the sky and say, "I'm leaving home. I swear to God I am," and I would just sit there a little scared, or I'd pull in my line and ask "How come?" I remember one time he said how he couldn't trust his own folks, and I said, "You mean your own mom and dad, you couldn't trust them? Then who could you trust?" He just looked away into the water and didn't talk as we fished through the afternoon or thought of another good story.

Then one day he had to move away. It was all part of the weird sad stories that hung on Kenny's life. You see, his father shot his mother in their kitchen, just shot her through the heart. He said he was cleaning a rifle and it went off, but how many times are we going to believe that one? The thing is, they were only about thirty years old, and already she was dead and he was sent to prison for manslaughter. And Kenny, he was shipped to Southern Ohio to live with his father's mother. I remember I looked up and there was Kenny's face on the tv as he stood in the doorway of his house looking out scared and alone as they interviewed his old aunt.

Of course we didn't go out fishing and talking after that. I'd maybe see Kenny downtown outside of the Palace Theatre, but we'd just nod, and then he moved away. It's the kind of story you see all the time on the Cleveland news, but it's never your own family or friends, and you're so glad, only this time it was.

I know I'm maybe a bit stupid or something else, but I really don't get it. I mean—How come? How come we all have to go around in fear and ignorance so much? And while you're at it—How come we have to drive by each other and just miss everyone so damn much?

FRIDAY

I lost my job today...for about an hour. That damn Cassandra, she makes me crazy sometimes, and this morning was one of them.

I admit it, I have trouble catching the bus. But it's not what you think. Like today, I stopped at the breakfast table to write in this. I was telling the story of Maria and me talking about life, and I had just gotten to the part about sitting through the sunset together. I had to finish it.

When I look up it is 6:35, and the bus comes at 6:30. I look up in time to hear its loud exhaust roaring around the corner. Holy Lorain! I say, which is an inside joke I have with this city. Holey Lorain! I sometimes say with an accent. Anyway, my bus is gone and Maria is still sleeping after a long night doing some project at The Wholesale Club, her second part-time job.

Though I know it is foolish, I talk myself into it. I will walk down 32nd Street out to the corner of Broadway, then head downtown. Someone I know will be driving to work and will pick me up. I'm a conditioned optimist.

The sun is breaking through and shining on the wet streets. But it is very quiet, even for 6:40, so I start to walk. I can do a pretty clip with my cane. You build a pace on a rhythm: stepidy—step/ stepidy-step/ stepidy-step. I'm passing by all the old storefronts, empty now or converted to tire and auto parts stores. I know to a stranger Lorain looks like a ghost town, a town with most of its teeth knocked out, but if you get close you can see more, you notice the little restaurant here, the used clothing store there, and even the town bars on the corners, the banks and offices—they're what's still here, what's going on.

And all the time I'm walking, I keep looking back at the faces of the drivers coming up. Some are dull, maybe just getting off their shift at Ford or the mill. They don't even look back, and I don't blame them. Some are young women with their faces and hair all done up—maybe waitresses or secretaries going in early to open up. They see me but look away quick like I was bad meat. Okay. Okay. Bless them, just the same, is what my grandmother Lorenz used to say, and it works.

It is a quarter till seven and I have another seven blocks. So I start hitchhiking, waving the old thumb in the air. You can get picked up for this in downtown Lorain, but I am already into desperate. Sweat is rolling down my cheeks and it is only 70 degrees by the bank thermometer. It is also 6:48.

Then I see her, my old girlfriend, Janet in her yellow Escort. She sees me too and, my gosh, she stops. I wasn't sure she would.

"Is that you, Marco?" she calls to me while winding down the passenger's window. I nod and she opens the door. There is no time to think of a way out, so I jump in. She smiles her sweet smile and in her high child's voice asks, "Well, how's the world treating you?"

I force a laugh and joke, "Just fine, like a lottery winner." She jolts surprise and I laugh, "Just kidding," tell her how I am late for work and beg, "Could you please drop me off downtown?"

"That's funny," she spurts, "I didn't know you could still work...with your leg and all." And she looks down at my leg which is just another leg in a pair of pants. She was always doing that, being thoughtlessly thoughtful. Believe me, it gets to be a heavy weight living around sweet Janet.

"I'm working at Rudy's Deli, for now," I say, and there is this heavy silence I didn't expect, so I add, "while I go to college at LCC." That's what everyone calls Lorain County Community College. I am stretching it a little here, but I am considering enrolling. I don't know what makes me lie to Janet. My father always said, "Tell a lie and everything becomes a lie; tell the truth and the whole world is true." I believe this, only right now I am just being human and confused.

"How've you been," I ask as she comes up to the red light. When I look over she is in tears, just bubbling over with them and gasping for breath. It is now 6:55, and I can see I am going to be late because she can't even see to drive now. "Pull over, Janet," I say, and she does in front of the bank at Henderson. All the other cars are whizzing past our window, when I touch her arm and whisper, "It's okay. It's okay to be sad."

And suddenly she jerks back, wipes her eyes on her handkerchief, and shifts into gear. We jerk out of there like a cat out of a box, giving me a minor whiplash, if there is such a thing.

"Oh, where did you say you worked...at Reni-Regi?"

"Janet, it's okay. I'll be late. I don't think you should keep driving when you're upset like this."

She doesn't even blink, only pushes forward, "I'm fine, really. Thank you. I don't know why I did that just now."

That is the very problem with Janet, she never really knows why she does *anything*. I always felt like she was some kind of head majorette listening to some inaudible music and leading me on.

We are at Broadway and Seventh, close enough. I reach over to touch her hand, "Janet, I'll get out right here." She is smiling that Janet smile once more as I mutter, "Thanks for the ride."

Some people you can't help because they don't know anything is wrong. Janet is an actress unto herself, "a real Telulah Bankhead" like my mother used to say. By the time I am turning down the alley behind Bobel's I hear myself saying, "Bless you, Janet." And the thing is I really mean it, and it works for me and I hope for Janet. I reach Rudy's back door at 7:10 and there in front of me is the witch Cassandra with her broom and boney face. I remember noticing that she is all in black.

"You're fired, you bum. Don't even come across that door," and she slams the back door in my face. I can see old Carlos is trying to plead my case, but by then she is pulling out her hair. I hear her scream something, but already I am at that place where I don't care. I care and don't, if you know what I mean. The worst has already happened and you're still there, you've survived. So I lean on the fence and laugh. I laugh for us all—for Maria up now and dressing for work, for Janet nosing her car into her parking spot at her father's furniture store, for Carlos shaking his head as he browns the homefries, and for Cassandra steaming herself into a fit over ten minutes. Suddenly I have all the time in the world, because it doesn't matter. What matters is everything and nothing; what matters is the morning air, the smell of the lake pouring into the Black River, the *caws* of the two seagulls in the parking lot, the faces of strangers as they drive by.

I just sat there in it and knew I would try and fail to write it all down, because some things are beyond words and yet you have to keep trying to put them down.

And when Rudy came out the back door around 8:00 looking for me, I was still there sitting in the grass along the back fence.

Wordless is how Cassandra and I were the rest of the day, till she sneezed and I said, "Bless you."

CALL WAITING

Maria didn't come home last night.
She didn't even call to lie her way around it. I know Esther warned me, so I guess I should have seen it coming. Should have seen it coming! Tell me, now when does anyone ever see it coming? Sure, now I can see all kinds of things—those long nights at work, her sleeping over at her sisters—Who was I kidding but myself? But, you see, I love that girl, and when did love ever serve as corrective lenses?

I fell asleep waiting at first, but then the cat wanted in, and then I was awake lying there listening for her car in the alley, her footsteps on the wooden stairs...down the hall. I'd fall asleep a moment and wake up thinking I'd missed it. So I got up and I made a few calls. Then about 3 am I started watching the tube in the dark—Bad movies and the shopper's network never helped anyone fall back asleep. Pretty soon I was riding the remote control, flicking around with each new thought.

It's not like Maria to just not call. Maybe something really bad happened and it hasn't been discovered yet. The police and the hospitals surely don't know anything, because I tried them twice. I don't think I can go to work. No heart. I just want to sit and listen to these sad songs with Otis Redding, feeling the time slip away.

Oh. Maria, Maria, Maria Concita Rosalita Gomez. Ave Maria, you're breaking my heart. Even your Mama tried to warn me. You crazy bird, I let you go. No one has ever written the song or poem to capture it—abandonment and loss—hurt and fear—they're just words, and writing them here brings no relief.

It's already morning. I'm calling off work and climbing back into bed. Let the sun move by itself today.

I am lying here listening to the sounds—the birds fighting around the feeder, the sputter of a car's engine, the roar of its exhaust, the rattle of someone kicking a garbage can. Neil Young is singing, "Only love can break your heart," and I am drinking the old port wine from the closet. I don't care, I am smoking in bed. It can all go straight to hell...all of you...my mother, my father, my sister already gone...Maria—go ahead, sneak away into the dark. I don't care anymore. I don't. I am falling asleep...

"Hello, hello. Maria, is that you? My God, where are you? Are you alright?"

"Marco, it's me, Maria. I'm in the hospital. I am okay, just shook up. I hit my head on the dashboard." I remember her voice trailed off like she was lost in pain or the medicine.

"Thank God, Maria. I can't tell you how glad I am to hear your voice."

"I drove our car into a ditch on Colorado Road, went right off and into a tree—that's the last I remember. Oh, my head is still throbbing. It was like a bad music video—the road, the tree, the lights, then the silence. They didn't find me till an hour ago. Some kid on a bike was going fishing. I forget his name."

My heart and my head are pounding, "Are you okay, Maria? Are you hurt anywhere?"

"Well, my arm and my head. They think one is broken, the other may be a con-cussion or something. Can you come get me soon? Call my mom, okay?"

"We'll be there as quick as the wind and your Mama's car can take us. Maria, I love you. Don't ever go away."

I pace around the kitchen, drink coffee without tasting it, then go out into the street to wait for Esther. Believe me, it happens that quick, the call that brings you back into life. Maria is okay. My life is okay. We are both alright now. Only the car is dead. We got through it again as we always do. Then why, oh God, do we give up so easy?

NO REPLY

I'm not answering the phone anymore. All we get are creditors and phone sales, and I hate hanging up on anyone. Maria brought home an old answering machine she bought at a garage sale. The first time we played it we heard the outgoing message of some stranger: "Hello, this is the Harper residence of Tom, Betty, and Susan. We're not home to take your message right now, but please leave your name...number...and the time you called at the tone, and we'll get back to you. Cheers." It was hilarious, and so original. Of course Maria had to make up a few wild messages for the Harpers, "Oh, Tom, I want you, I need you, I lo-love you...with all my hate." But me, I started imagining their tired suburban life, and erased the thing.

Now when the phone rings I have to get to it before our voice message comes on. I get three rings—it's like a little timebomb we brought into our house. Maria says, "Just let it play," but I can't stand not answering. I've barked my shins more than once on the coffee table getting to it from across the room. Maria can just stand there as their voice comes on, "Hello, this is Carol from the loan department of Huntington Bank." But I have to pick it up or walk away.

Maria did our message which starts out with our cat Babs crying as Maria sings, "Yes, we have no bananas. This is 543-2111. You know what to do. Do it and we may get back to you cause... We have no bananas to-day!" It's cute.

I tell you, I really can't stand this always having no money. Our paychecks are already gone before they arrive. Besides rent and utilities, we've got Maria's Emergency Room bills still coming in and no health insurance, and we are 'sans machina,' without a car. Maria's brother would lend us his Ford Ranger if he could start it, says it needs a new engine—don't we all. We talked about it and Maria said tomorrow she's going down to get food stamps. When I said I hate it, she looked me in the eyes and asked, "Haven't you been paying taxes most of your life? Who else are they for?" We swore we'd get off them as soon as something breaks for us, but what?

Yesterday Maria came home to find me sitting at the kitchen table staring at our stack of bills which seemed to be rising like a brick wall. "Why aren't you writing?" she asked looking right into my face. I said nothing, just nodded at the pile of paper. Then Maria did a real Maria thing—she just leaned toward me like she was about to give me a kiss but instead she blew all those bills right onto the floor. "There!" she said, "Now go and write!"

We left them there the rest of the night. After making love around Midnight we listened to Neil Young's *Harvest Moon* tape. I like the line about "Just like children sleepin'/ We could dream this night away." I was feeling calm and restful inside when I said it, "Maria, I've got it. Tomorrow we will pay the first bill we pick up."

Maria laughed and threw off the sheet. She climbed across me and was still sweating as she leaned down to kiss my eyes. I swear her breasts were moons. "Now, Marco, you're getting it."

"I *know* I am," I laughed, my head thrown back on my arms.

Just then the phone started to ring, and Maria just smiled wide as she began rocking her hips into mine. Believe me, this time I let the machine take it.

222 BAR MEMORY

I've decided to go way back for this one, to try and remember how things were back when Mom and Dad were alive and still with me.

My father used to take me down to his favorite bar on the corner of Grove Avenue and 28th Street. It was in the daytime and the bar was near the millgate, so lots of his buddies from the rolling mill would come in. He'd buy them a drink, or they'd buy him one. I was about 6 then, his boy. "So this is your boy?" they'd shout and slap his back or mine, making big millworkers' grins. I knew then that I was one of them, had become a part of their place.

When I got older, junior high age, Dad would set me up in a store across the street with a coke and a comic book He would go into 222 Bar for a couple drinks. I remember Dad said I was too old and too young to be going in there. It was about the same time that the mill was taken over by US Steel.

Anyway what I remember as a kid is how warm and friendly it all was. Those guys would talk about how the mill was running, how the Browns or Indians were doing, or where fish were biting. There were all these picture of great sports figures on the walls, and the pool balls would be clicking in the back. I'd just sit there in the rock 'n' roll music and the soft light of beer signs. It was a regular melting pot— mostly Pollocks and Italians, Hungarians and Slovaks, but also Puerto Ricans and Blacks. It was a regular mill bar.

I think I saw a couple of fights there as a kid, but they were both over women. My dad would shake his head and say he just couldn't understand it, and we'd be heading for the door. "Not a word of this to your mother. Understand?"

They say back in the sixties and seventies over 14,000 men and women worked in those mills. "Prosperity" was a big word back then. *Prosperity*—someone would get a new car or have an outboard parked in front of the garage, and everyone would smile and say, "It's prosperity!" I remember it was around 1980 that we first noticed it— *the change.* There are always rumors in a milltown, always fears and dreams, but in 1980 you started actually seeing guys in their early 60's retiring, hanging around the house, out working in their yard, or walking their dog. Pretty soon, they'd buy a camping trailer and head south. At first we thought this too was *prosperity.* "It must be prosperity," my Aunt Mary said when her husband retired early. It was actually called a *buy-out,* where the company would get the older men to retire early by giving them a few years toward their retirement benefits.

When Dad got the word that they wanted to buy him out, he didn't want to do it. "What did I do wrong?" he asked one night at the table. I remember later sitting with him out on the front porch drinking beers. I was almost 20 then, and we just sat on the metal chairs watching people and cars go by for a long time. Then Dad sat his beer hard on the cement floor and cursed, "Shit! That's what it is. A big old crock of it!" His face was red and his lips were shaking. "Son, I'll tell you the truth—they gave me the axe today; that's what they did." I'd never seen my dad upset like this where his hand was shaking as he pointed toward the sky. "I been there since it was National Tube back in the 1950's. Damn! A man works 30 years, see, gives them 30 back breaking years, and they say, 'Thanks but you can go. We don't need you around here no more. So long!'—just like that," and he spit into the grass. "No, they don't even say that. It's just a little meeting where they hand you a sheet with a bunch of numbers and a red line showing where you're ready to be *let go*. Damn it all to hell and back!"

"It's okay, Dad." I tried to comfort, then blurted out, "You're better than they are, anyway."

I didn't know what to say, but he just looked at me and snapped, "No, ain't nobody better than nobody else in this! There ain't, you hear?" His face was beet red, and his hands were shaking. When he calmed down a bit, he held my arm and spoke softly, "Son, the problem is there ain't nobody doing this. It's all worked out that way. It ain't the mill and it ain't your bosses or your fellow workers, 'cause they're just doing what they're told, and they'll be the next to go and they know it."

I kept my silence, sipping beer and getting dizzy trying to figure it all out. He looked right at me, "Let me ask you something, Marco—Who owns these mills? Who *owns* them? Is it anyone who lives near here, is it anyone who works in them? No, it ain't and it's a sad time when no one is here to account. The owners, boy, are corporations far from here who have nothing to lose. We're just loose change in their pockets. And when someone finally closes us down, the owners will have long ago sold us off. No, when you don't hurt with the mill, you don't own it. You understand? It's not theirs to sacrifice." His eyes were big mirrors.

"Yeah, I think I do, Dad."

"Well, never forget it, Marco, 'cause you are more than your work. But, your *work*...Your work is a part of your life." He stared right at me, and I tell you, I could *feel* his eyes grow wet.

I don't remember what we did after that. I probably went up to my room and read something. I do remember that about a month later, the day after my 21st birthday, I talked him into going with me to the 222 Bar. I thought it would do some good to get him back around his buddies. But, it didn't. His friends would come in and we'd see them look away. Or maybe they'd wave and go sit down at the bar. The looks on their faces, the shame or pity or grief that cut across their eyes—I wanted to bust them one, start a big fight, but I looked over and Dad was finishing his drink.

"It's okay, son" he said. "It's okay. What else can they do?" He was at a place where he could accept it, while I couldn't. Then he touched my arm and whispered, "Let's get out of here."

He drove us over to The French Creek Park down by the Black River. It was just getting dark and we sat at a picnic table and drank away our 8-pack of Black Label. I remember we talked things and watched the kids in the park as he named the birds in the trees.

How come I'm telling all this? I'll tell you. 14,000 men and women once worked in these Lorain mills. And now it takes just 2,000 workers breaking their backs and hearts to keep that dinosaur alive.

MAKING WAVES

We are in a van cruising around the curves of Route 90 going into Cleveland. José called to say they needed people at the Indians game today. They are making a protest again in front of the new stadium—"We Don't Want Chief Wahoo! Wahoo Has to Go!"

Now, I'm thinking you may not be from Cleveland and may not know that Wahoo is this big grinning Indian face which Cleveland Indians fans love but which affronts anyone Native American. I'm not, but José is, and so is Maria in part. "We're all part Apache," José reminds them. "Our Mexican grandfather married our Apache grandmother, so we are all their hybrid crop." He usually says it with a loud laugh, as though he's a proud father. But in his tired face I've also read real anger. His body is quiet but his eyes look around quick and his lips thin, though covered with a thick mustache. Believe me, it's not Chief Wahoo's face.

I come along for the ride, and because they need the numbers.

It's a Saturday morning, around ten, and we are all packed into this van like buns in a bag. Maria is leaning onto my shoulder, and her round sleepy face presses softly into my jacket sleeve. I'd like to be sleeping beside her on this our day off, and wake to coffee and bacon and eggs at the kitchen table. But here is where we are.

"Where do we meet José?" asks Maria's brother for the third time. "At the stadium parking lot," he answers himself. He's fifteen and nervous.

"Right," the driver shouts. "At noon—Gateway Parking Lot." And the van winds under an overpass and rises up around the curve that opens the Cleveland skyline. Above the industrial foreground of the West Side and beneath the clouds that circle Lake Erie, are the three towers: Terminal, BP, and Society. The sun makes everything right. "Cleveland—5 Miles," flashes from the bridge overhead.

The last time we rode in with José, he sang most of the way..."Juan Tanemara" his favorite, but also Native and Mexican songs. Maria sings too, and he calls her his Little Chihuahua and they laugh.

One time José told me the story of why he moved to Cleveland. He was living in Sandusky, a lake town to the west. He and his wife, Rene, were working at the K-Mart and living on a little rented farm at the edge of town.

"My sons Adrian and Patrick are twins, you know," and he pointed to their round faces in the back seat. Two boys with beautiful black hair smiled back at us. "See the long hair."

"Yes," I nodded. "It's great."

"Well, it gets them in trouble. Doesn't it, boys? Big trouble." And they both laughed and tickeled each other. "The schools, Marco. The schools kicked them out because their hair was too long."

"You're kidding," was all I could think to say. "How?"

"Well, they called Rene and me at the K-Mart where we were working. 'We have a problem,' was all they would say, 'Come in and maybe we can clear this thing up,' that's what the principal said, but believe me nothing is that simple unless it's the white person's mind."

José was heating up as he talked, his eyes were watching the road, but you could watch the wheels turning in his head. "All that son of a bitch wanted was for the boys to just cut off all their hair and be white. You know, Marco, we Indian people cut our hair only at times of death and mourning. It was a violation he was asking of us, but he didn't see any of it. 'I'm sure you'll see we have the same rules for all of our children,' he repeated. And I said something like that might be your problem, but he didn't get that either, never would. 'Boy's hair must be no longer than their collar.' 'What,' I said, and he answered again, 'The collar is the test, you see,' like it made any sense."

"Now, Marco, did you ever hear anything like this? 'The collar is the test,' as if those were God's words. All my life I been dealing with this bullshit. Someone feels they have power and they make a definition. It's 'the collar' or 'Chief Wahoo' or 'Indian' or 'Chicano' or 'the underclass.' See, Marco, people are always drawing these damn lines separating us from each other, and what they don't know is that what it really does is divide themselves." I just sat and listened as he rolled his eyes and sighed. "Marco, all they know is to recite what things are, and it's because they fear something, and that something is also themselves."

He was looking hard into my eyes then, and I was thinking of all the ways I did that too, that definition thing. "I know what you're saying, José." We both looked out the window. It was starting to rain.

"So I said to this principal, his fat white face staring down at me from his desk, I said, 'I understand, sir. But you know, of course, that their hair is part of their culture. It's part of their religion.' I could see he wasn't getting any of it, so I spoke through the pain in his face, 'It's their right, man. It's called freedom of religion.' And he yells back, 'This is a public school!' and I stood up and I declared, 'Man, I will fight you on this.'

"Well I did for a while, for a long while. We kept the boys out of school for a couple weeks, then we enrolled them in Holy Angels Catholic School on Sandusky's West Side. The priest there understood, only we couldn't afford the tuition, and I didn't want to be living in Sandusky no more, so we moved to Cleveland." In the back seat the boys were cheering and shouting: "It's their *right*, man," and "Man, I will *fight* you on this."

I look up as our van is crossing the bridge over the Flats, that huge industrial wasteland. Then we are pulling into the parking lot off Ontario Street. José and his boys are already there with their signs being blown by the lake wind. They hold on, looking out at the traffic. They are wearing red shiny jackets and long braided hair. Their sisters in bright skirts are dancing in a circle of sun, so I lean over and kiss Maria's eyes. "Maria...Wake up," I call, "It's time to begin."

QUICK RETURNS

Maria comes back from work at 9:45. She parks the truck out in the street and lets the screen door slam hard.

"We're victims of middle management," she says and sits down hard at the table. "They let me go, Marco. Compu-Graphics let me go. I'm fired." She tries to force a laugh but gets tears instead, and I am kneeling beside her brushing her hair with my palm.

Suddenly she pulls back, stands up and pours a cup of coffee into her morning cup. I hand her the cream.

"What they did was bring me into the office and Tom hands he a pink slip to read, 'Compu-Graphics has begun a program of reconfiguring its parttime employment situation based on work-study data and new demographics.' What is this shit?" she bursts out and I can see her face grow flush, anger bubbling up through tears. "Barbara says they're either hiring someone's daughter for the summer or going belly up. I'd rather they said *that* than this business *mumbo-jumbo.*"

I want to hold and kiss her, but wait while she walks around the room. "I tell you. I'll go and work for my uncle Luis running book in the Mexican lottery."

She doesn't mean it, so I joke, "How about if we just win the lottery instead?" I cannot tell her yet that our landlord Bob has stopped by. He came soon afdter she left for work. This is Wednesday, my day off. I can't tell her that we have to move. We live in this old brick house on Toledo Avenue with three other families—the Jarmans, the Jurasicks, and Frank and Ted. Bob said that's the problem—too many people for one house. The building inspector has told him one family has to go. Since we're the last in, we're the first to go out the door. I need to tell her this, but can't, and suddenly that cliff's edge of homelessness is at my feet and I have to sit down. We sit like that for a long time, silent, breathing, listening, and waiting. The radio is playing old songs. Then Maria reaches across the table to my hand. She is smiling as the sun comes through the kitchen curtains onto her bare arms, her dark hair.

"Marco," she says softly, "In about an hour we are going out to buy the papers. Then I will sit and go through till I find another job. If nothing else, I hear they're hiring at the new Super-K. Anyway, for now I'm taking your hand and leading you into our little bedroom where we will hold each other and keep our hearts warm."

I am still in my pajamas, and Maria is in her office clothes, but we lie down together in the music, make soft love for an hour, wake in each other's arms.

Around noon we come back with the papers and find a note taped to the door. It says, "Marco and Maria, We missed you two, hope you won't miss us too much, but we're moving out, moving in with friends. Don't be strangers." It was signed, "Frank and Ted."

Maria looks up to ask me please, what is this about, and I begin again.

GOOD NEWS TUESDAY

I have to write this down, because I don't want to forget. It's called "The Ohio Board of Rehabilitation" and they have offices in Cleveland. I'm going to call them first thing Monday, even if I have to take off work. Mack, the guy who runs the Jolly Donut, told me about it about an hour ago. He acted like I was lost or something for not knowing about it, but who was I to ask? I don't have a doctor anymore, and besides it doesn't pay for medical just for retraining, I think.

You see, I had seen that Mack wore this metal brace on his lower leg. He doesn't show it, but anyone who has a limp can recognize another. Well, I was sitting there staring out the window at the morning traffic and half listening to Ron, the guitar salesman, talk about his latest gig. When he said he was writing song lyrics, I told him that I was a writer too. Everybody at the table looked around at me like I'd just said I found a mouse in my coffee.

"What kind of writing?" Tom asked.

"What's it matter?" Ron said, trying to bring the attention back to himself. "Anyway, I was ..."

"No, I want to know what kind of writing Marco is doing so that he calls himself a writer. Do you mind?"

I really didn't want to get into it, but I figured I'd say it and get it over with. "I'm writing my life story."

"Bull-shit!" It was Ron this time. "What kind of life you got to write about?"

"Well, I know I ain't among 'America's Most Wanted,'" I joked.

"And you sure as hell ain't among 'The Rich and Famous,'" laughed Ron.

"Well, hey," I shouted, "I got a life and it's the only thing I know to write about." I hadn't planned on saying all that. "Well put, my man." It was Mack who had been wiping the table next to us. "I require of every writer, first or last, a simple and sincere account of his own life."

"*What?*" It was Tom setting down his coffee cup.

"It's a line from Henry David Thoreau, the fellow that went into the woods to 'suck all the marrow of life,'" Mack answered back, leaning on our table now with its line of empty cups and stacks of cigarette butts in both ashtrays. "Come on, you guys can talk all morning about the politics of this town. Can't you get into what Marco's saying: Speak your life. That's what he's doing. Right?"

And I knew he was going to turn to me just then and I'd have to take the ball and run with it. "That's it. See, I used to write stories, made up things about murders and sex and space creatures. Then I didn't write nothing for a long time, but now I'm writing again, and what I'm writing is the truth of my life."

"You writing about us here at Jolly Donut?" It was Ron this time, and I said no, but I guess that would now be a lie. I'm just writing things that come up, sketching it down in this here Big Chief notebook, then working them up on Maria's typewriter.

"Where you publishing them?" asked Tom.

"Nowhere, Tom. It's just what I do. I didn't mean to get you guys all riled up over this. I was just giving you a 'sincere account' of my life." They laughed, and then we all got quiet.

But Mack was feeling generous, so he went and got the coffee pot, and said, "Well, Marco, the coffee is hot, so let's hear some of your life story. Right now, and right here," and he began to pour all around.

I read them the one about "222 Bar" because I knew that they knew the place and my old man. And I swear, as I was laying it in about the way the mills shut down old Lorain, they were all nodding and cursing, cheering me on. It was like the old days in Lorain High School, when I would read stories to my buddies after lunch. And when I was done, there was this silence, then Tom reached out his hand and said, "Let me shake the hand of a writer."

It was a really good time, where I could feel the story's own truth and know that I was being a witness somehow. I had to be true to the life, and the life would then pay me back.

I had to promise them I'd read another tomorrow, and as they headed off to their separate days, I felt someone's hand on my shoulder. "Sit down," Mack said. "Come on, sit down for a minute, man." So I did, even though Maria would be wondering where I was with the bread and eggs.

"Marco, listen, did you ever think about studying writing? I don't mean grammar. I mean creative writing at some college?"

"Are you kidding me, Mack? Where am I going to get any money to go to college. I'm just making enough now to pay the rent and buy—bread and eggs. That's it. Maria and I together can't even buy a decent car."

"Yeah, I know that story, man. But you don't know the whole story. See, there are government programs for folks just like you and me. They helped me get the loan to open this place, and if I'm not wrong, they'll help you go to college to learn to write."

I looked into his face and there was no mistaking it.

"I don't know," I said, shaking my head. "How do you know I qualify?"

He looked at my leg and patted his own. "It's our wounds, Marco. We bear them and they bear us. Give yourself that break. Stop resisting your fate. It only causes you pain."

That's when he gave me that name—the Ohio Board of Rehabilitation and a number in Cleveland to call. I'm telling you, it all feels like a dream right now, a door without a lock. But the best part is not this new hope but the old connection, those guys eating up my writing at the Jolly Donuts.

GETTING SOME CLASS

When I got off the bus last night—from working the late shift—I felt this chill in the air. It was the bite of fall in the September air. I knew it like my own hand, only tonight it felt strange like I was walking and could see myself walking at the same time. I looked back down Broadway toward the "Journal" building, right where the road turns, and I felt something like loss, like watching my dad and my mom and my brother being carried away. I was there and I was not. Only the traffic light signalled life, and I turned down 28th street shuffling home quick.

When I got home Maria was already asleep, so I wrote this down and crawled in warm beside her. But I remember, that traffic light burned on my eyelids as I fell into sleep.

Maria drove me out here. She left me here at the door of the community college, and said she had to visit her sisters and pick up groceries, but I could tell she was afraid. So I held her hard before getting out. "You do good at school, Marco," she said, "'cause I love you," then drove away. She couldn't know how afraid I was or how much she means to me.

It was my first class, "Introduction to Creative Writing," and it was taught by Dr. Franco, a young bearded Greek guy with a gentle way of speaking to everyone. I honestly thought I would be the only older one, but you wouldn't believe the people in here: one is a mortician, another a librarian's assistant, several mothers, one woman who's a waitress at Rudy's Cafe, a guy who's easily seventy and has a lot to say—but good stuff really. There's also a Swedish cook from the Holiday Inn, about eight nineteen-year-olds, and me, Marco the writer.

The first night Dr. Franco explained how there are stages of being a writer. That for a long time you only think about being one; you know, where you're always thinking about writing but never actually doing it—the "I have this great idea for a story" stage, he called it. Then you tell yourself you are a writer and struggle to convince yourself, but it's good because now you're actually doing some writing; then you become a writer to yourself and others by being published somewhere. But it doesn't end there. Because then all you want to do is write and when you're not writing, it's bugging you. "In the end," he said, giving us all a serious eye, "you don't choose writing; it chooses you. You do it because you have to."

I never heard anybody talk so true about it. Like this feeling is so real others have it. I didn't say anything, but I think I passed into the have to do it stage way back when I was in junior high, and I've been doing it ever since like eating or drinking or breathing each day.

He passed out some papers on how we were to submit things to the workshop and how it would be run. You hand in something you're writing on, and he runs it off on a "worksheet," and the night of class you read it outloud, and the others tell you what they think about it. A nervous laughter spread around the room. Then we read a poem and a story by Ernest Hemingway and Dr. Franco tried to get us to talk about it, only we made him do most of the talking.

When we took a break I could hear the young ones worrying about what they would give him for the worksheet. The older women over by the coffee machine were already scared and thinking about dropping. I went outside in the crisp night air and stood under the big lamp and had a smoke with the Sweedish cook. I asked him what he thought, and he smiled and said, "It's nice." I wanted to tell him how my heart was beating like a drum because my life had suddenly been plugged in, but I didn't. I just nodded and said, "Yeah. Nice."

When Maria picked me up I didn't get in. Instead I made her get out and walk around the buildings with me. It was almost ten o'clock, and she did have milk in the car, but we walked together down hallways and up stairs, looking in rooms, and then we had a coffee back at the school's little restaurant which the college development guy showed me. We talked and then we watched in silence, and then we drove home together and made love to the music of Gloria Estefan— all of it warm and real.

TELLING IT

On Friday Dr. Franco (I hate the name, but I love the guy) told us to write a story that involved research. "I want you to see the truth that lies in facts," he said. On my last paper he wrote, "Great characters, Marco. Now give it more plot." To the whole class he said, "This should be a story with *tensions*—not just conflict, but *necessary oppositions*." I am not sure what he meant by that, but I knew the story that had brought me there, the one I had been waiting eight years to write.

This weekend Maria is away at her mother's. Esther has been having trouble with her gallstones and so is going into the hospital to have them pulverized. Strange to think how something so violent could help you to heal. It never worked that way for me. I have to struggle to learn anything. Anyway, it is just me and the cats all weekend with no car, so I am settling into writing this Saturday morning with my coffee and my shoebox of research on the floor. The shoebox goes back to June 1987 where this story begins. It once held the steeltoed boots that I bought for working in the mill.

I had just gotten my call that they were hiring me in. I took the mill physical at Saint Joseph's Hospital and was to report to the rolling mill on Monday. I was in! I remember that Friday morning going out to my brother Ted's house on Homewood. He was sitting at the kitchen table when I told him, "Look out, Big Brother, I may be working beside you soon." He looked up from his coffee, and his eyes were happy but his mouth was sad. Calmly he leaned forward, "Marco, I hate to tell you this, really, but we're going to strike.

We've given away all our concessions, and USX ain't even listening to our demands." I remember I stood there at his kitchen table for a long moment swallowing my good news, caught between knowing Ted was right and wanting my own break at a job. The television was blasting in the other room, and Ted stood up and pulled a bill from his wallet. "Here's a twenty. Buy your shoes," is all he said, and so I did, and I waited.

The rest of the stuff in the box are the clippings from the newspapers during the strike of '87. See, even though I don't like to talk about it and don't claim to understand it, I have always known it was a climactic time in my life, like the busted knee cap that left me crippled, a pivotal point for my own story which I am writing here.

It was a particularly cold November with a thin layer of snow on the ground that week. The Great Steel Strike in Lorain had gone on for over one hundred and twenty days, some kind of national record. Only the United Steelworkers' Union didn't call it a "strike"; they called it a "lockout." USX the new division name for the United Steel Company called it a "strike." Men stood around the picket barrels and joked about it's being "one hell of a Thanksgiving this year." Though they wouldn't talk about it, many had become house husbands, sitting around the place waiting for their kids to come home from school, their wives to come home from part-time jobs at K-Marts or the Midway Mall. They hated it, playing that game of solitaire. Standing around the picket barrels or sitting in Rudy's Deli they felt better and talked mostly about the Cleveland Browns, about plans to go ice fishing up on Sandusky Bay or deer hunting around Wellington. Only this year the fishing and hunting had some urgency around it. As much as the family needed the food, the men needed to provide it.

I had worked exactly three days in the mill, on a track gang around the blast furnace—"a brief and bright career," we joked, but it was not enough to get me into the union or to collect any benefits. I went back to making deliveries for Miller's Applaince part time; I was used to that. But I could see how the strike's gradual wearing away of income hit Ted's family. It comes in little ways: not going out to eat or to the movies at first, canceling the cable tv, then it gets to not eating good meat everyday—bring out the macaroni and cheese—then telling the kids no to everything they ask for, wearing the same old clothes, running garage sales in November for neighbors without money, husbands and wives fighting at the kitchen sink, the men mostly sneaking off to bars in the days. As a mill kid, I'd lived through many strikes. It was kind of like having a bad year at school where some teacher hates you, and your parents go in and talk, then tell you to "Just get through this year." But I'll tell you something about a strike—you never get used to it.

One day I went out to Ted's house, and his wife Marge was in the kitchen breading fish, I mean boxes of it. "Hey, Marco, come on in. The coffee's on the stove." She stepped back from the table and took a quick drag on her cigarette. Marge is a big woman, but she loves doing things, and fixing food is tops on her list. That day her hair was covered with a blue kerchief and her hands were busy slapping down the fish. Her eyes were soft but full of light as she spoke, "The Union Auxillary is having a fish fry, and you're just in time to give us a hand carrying these out to the van."

"How's it going, Marge?" I asked, pouring us both a cup of coffee, mine in a Browns cup, hers in a mug marked "Solidarity."

"Marco," she said looking straight through me, "I don't care. I love this town." She was having a good day. "I mean this lockout brings it out. Do you know every automotive shop in town is giving free repairs. And the donut and pizza shops are giving the pickets free food, bringing it right out to the lines." All the time she was slapping the fish throught he batter. "Last week, Marco, our auction raised $2,000."

This work had come to mean so much to her. She needed to believe in something. "That's great," I said, nodding into my cup. "I came down Broadway and could see fellows handing out fliers saying 'Don't Buy Marathon Gas—It's US Steel.'" I chuckled, "Do you really think it makes any difference?"

"It does in this house," she said, staring down at the pale fish slabs all over the table—a sad school for fish.

I remembered why I had come, "Where's Ted?"

"Out at the Ford plant. They're doing a gate collection out there all day. You know we got $6,000 from the plant over in Brunswick." She sat her cup back down on the counter and started breading fish again. "Marco, for now, this is what we've got, and it does make a difference to us."

"I know," I said, finishing my coffee. She reminded me so much of my mother standing there. That afternoon I started loading the boxes into the van, and stuck around to drive them over to the church. In the evening I had all the fish I ever cared to eat.

Thanksgiving week things really started to happen. The Union had already allowed some contractors into the mills to do some repair work—as long as there was no wage roll work going on. But then the company said they wanted to ship some pipe that had been made before the strike (lockout) had begun. The Union said no, but then some judge from Cuyahoga County had issued a preliminary injunction against the Union's blocking the shipment. It was judge Frank Gorman from Cleveland, not our own Judge Beteski, who would have known what this meant to tired and hungry steelworkers. "We're Lean and Mean," one picket read, only the good judge didn't see it, because I guess he was off having dinner at some fancy place in Shaker Heights. Anyway, it was like striking a match, where everyone waits to see what's going to catch fire.

My brother called me over to his place that Monday night. He was sitting in the kitchen putting on his work boots when I got there. "Well, brother," he said, "I want you to come with me tonight. You better learn something about the union if you want to make the mill your life." Ted always felt I should go off to Kent State and learn to be a teacher or something, only he never knew where I should get the money. "We're going over to the union hall to plan our response to this damn injunction. Okay?" And he looked up to my grinning face. "I'll bring you in with me. It'll be okay. I want you should hear this."

We drove past the pickets on the corner of Grove and 28th Street, right along side of the closed mill, a sleeping bear in the dark. The union hall on Broadway was noisy around nine at night, but it was good to see these folks you'd see quiet on the streets, alive and boasting together here. All these great ethnic faces, Lorain's salad bowl collected here. The women among them had sharp and determined eyes. Older fellows who'd retired were sitting in the back sipping coffee from styrofoam cups. Somebody joked, "This looks like the International Festival!"

When the Union's Local President Al Pena and District Director Frank Valenta took the stage at about 9:20, the crowd settled down. A woman representative stepped up to the microphone and started them singing—this big crowd were suddenly singing about union brother and sisterhood, as if they were singing the national anthem at their kid's football game. Then someone up front started us chanting "Solidarity—Forever" till the whole place roared, "Solidarity—Forever."

Ted leaned over to ask, "What do you think, little brother?"and I just nodded as they clapped.

Pena was a dark husky man, famous in this town as the first Hispanic to hold the rank of President. He began by praising them for hanging on through hard times. Then he read some letters from other locals around the country. "All of these are coming in with checks to help us carry on." He shouted "You men and women of USW Lorain Works are a symbol that unions are still alive in this country," and the crowd roared. "I worked in every division of this mill for 25 years, and I know the quality of workers we have. It's too damn bad the company doesn't." I began to hear something, how the workers separated the 'mill' from the 'company' when they talked, how one provided, the other took away. Only the company was damned.

Pena spoke with such assurance it quieted everyone. He remembered "The great national steel strike of 1950—when all the unions bonded together to shut them down."

"I was a young man then...and now I'm 65," he told them, "And you know what? You know what? The unions and the workers will survive." It was the greatest speech I'd ever heard because it was so real and important. I looked around at the faces. We'd all had a blood transfusion.

Valenta got up and sketched in the situation, told how the talks were stalled, how US Steel was now so diversified, they could afford to hurt themselves a little just to break our backs. Someone shouted "Hell, they own parts of Marathon and Texas Oil." Then Valenta called for the men to be there for picket duty, for them to remain nonviolent, but to remember "We ain't going to allow any shipment of steel out of this plant if we can help it. Our kids are hungry and we're not working. Stand together." A roar went up followed by a chanting of "Stand Together—Stand Together!"

Ted pulled my sleeve, "Let's get out of here before the crowd," and we pushed our way back through the others and out into the cool air where the lights of the parking lot spread on new fallen snow. "That..." he said, "is what union spirit is all about," and we laughed together in the quiet car, like we were kids again before a game of street football. Heading to his place for a beer I turned the music down for a moment and said, "Dad should have been here." Ted just nodded beside me and said that he was.

That was Monday.

Tuesday night Ted called to say he had pulled a picket shift at the Sheffield Village railroad crossing for Wednesday noon. "You're not part of the union and really can't picket," he said, "but I wondered if you wanted to come along and wait in the car."

"Sure," I said, without needing to think.

Wednesday morning he came to pick me up around 11:00. Instead of just honking, he came into my apartment and his face was all serious, tight lines around his eyes as he stared into my face.

"What's up?" I asked reaching for my coat.

"Wait," he said, catching my arm, "You may not want to be in on this one." His grip was hard.

"What is it, brother?"

"The word is that USX will be shipping that load of pipe out through the tracks on East River Road where we're headed. There's going to be some kind of confrontation. They've already piled stones on the tracks, and the call has gone out to everyone who's not on duty elsewhere to be on call." All I could do was listen, then Ted confessed, "This could be it."

I waited a moment thinking of what all "it" meant, then looked again into his face which kept saying, "It's up to you, Marco." I grabbed my coat and hat.

We parked our car at French Creek Park and walked up East River Road. There were guys inside the Cliff House Tavern drinking and watching at the windows. More were sitting in cars drinking coffee all along the road. Ted knew some of them. We were only allowed 16 official picketers at each site; these guys were the unofficial. I was just going to walk up close enough for a good look.

We walked past the houses on Wright Avenue. I could spot a few faces of kids at the window curtains. At the crossing, we could see the burn barrel and a circle of men in coats and Union jackets. The sky was gray and a layer of mist lay on everything. On the tracks were a huge pile of rocks and an old rusted car. I think it was a Fiat. It was hard to tell because it was lying upside down on its roof, with an American flag sticking out of its exhaust. Someone had set an old yellow couch right across the tracks, and two guys were sitting on it. Others were still carrying picket signs; some were leaning up against the fence. One guy was telling another how to dismantle the train engine by cutting the hoses. "I'm an engineer on that train," he said, "I should know how to shut her down."

Suddenly a man with a cordless phone yelled, "The train is moving out of the mill. Bill's down at Seneca Avenue. The shipment is headed our way...with a regiment of police. He says they came in through the Pearl Avenue gate."

Some kind of siren went off, and a guy with a battery megaphone started talking, "They're bringing the shipment out. They're bringing the shipment out. It's time. It's time." He kept talking double like that, making sure we heard, giving us time for it to sink in.

I looked at Ted and he at me, "For what?" I said.

"Man, I don't know. You better get back from here. Something big is going down."

"Not on your life," I said. "I'm here because I'm here. I ain't going away."

Guys started streaming out of their cars. I recognized two of them as Pena and Valenta. There were over a hundred of us. The guy spoke through the megaphone, "Let's assemble up here; they ain't going to run us through, by God." There seemed some question in that statement, but the crowd followed orders. By then we could see the train heading our way, and he was right, the police were everywhere. Unbelievable. Cops with dogs and rifles, wearing riot gear of helmets and clubs were walking out with the damn train from inside the mill. "Son of a bitch! Bunch of hired goons!" one guy yelled.

Ted said, "They're on company property...makes them hired goons." We stood our ground as they marched steadily towards us. Television crews stood on the sidelines waiting and rolling. I felt this huge sense burning in me that I was being a public witness. This was a moment to remember and record.

Right before noon several cruisers came down 31st Street followed by an empty bus. Snipers with rifles were spotted up on the roofs. "It's a Goddamn civil war," somebody shouted. And as the police got close we could see that some were the local and county police—guys we all knew—and some were from the sheriff's office of Huron County. There were more than a hundred.

"Where's mayor Olejko?" somebody shouted, "Where is he now? We elected him,and where is he now!" The police started forming a line at the intersection, and someone recognized a friend, "Lou, what are you doing over there!" he shouted, but Lou just held to his club and looked away. There were about three hundred of us—workers and police—all about the same age gathered on East River Road for a battle. On the tracks up front were Pena or Valenta arm and arm, and they kept telling the men, "No violence, but stand together. Remember, no violence. If anyone gets arrested, let it be us."

Someone shouted, "This has gone too far."

Someone for the police, maybe it was Sheriff Mahoney, spoke over their megaphone, "You must break up this assembly."

"Go home, traitors," came from the other side.

"You are breaking the law right now."

And the obscenities started pouring from the crowd.

"You men are breaking the law and will be arrested," the megaphone snarled back. Ted and I were being crowded back from the road and onto the mill property along the tracks, near the overturned car.

You could see the police were getting worried now. They were young faces like our own. Someone shouted, "This ain't no Kent State!" The cop at the megaphone answered back, "This shipment is going through," and the crowd went wild. They started throwing more than words, as the train engine spread its light upon us. "You're all under arrest," shouted a sheriff, "Take them, men!" Suddenly someone grabbed Pena and pulled him from us. He stood strong but refused to fight. They were wrestling him to the ground beside the tracks. Three guys tried to handcuff him behind his back while a fourth guy bent over and started jabbing him in the back with his billy club. Valenta was shouting then and dashed towards them. He was pushed away but he came back, catching a billy club right in the face. Whack! I swear you could hear the bones cracking. For a moment everyone stood stunned—as if watching a movie, as if it was too large to be true. Then a wild roar went up as the strikers began shoving back.

Now this is the part that's so hard for me to get right, because it's so important yet I can't remember it. The train had stopped by then, but the shoving had grown worse. Waves of workers and cops bled into each other. People were falling on the ground. It was like the cops beating Blacks in Selma or something. We stumbled over our own feet. Ted rolled down the bank near the Black River, and as I turned to reach for him I heard this thump, followed by a quick crack, and reached down for my knee, but it wasn't there any more, just a leg gone horribly wrong. I doubled over and landed on the sharp pain of it. I heard the hiss of the train's brakes and against a spotlight saw a gray shirted cop running with his club held high. That was all.

When I awakened in Saint Joseph's Hospital, I was told by a young intern that I had shattered my knee cap. "I had shattered" rang in my head as a nausea forced me to turn away from his innocent, stupid face. "Shattered," I whispered to myself. "Shattered." It rung through my life.

That's the story of how my leg was ruined, though it isn't all of it. There in the box is also the story of those days after the confrontation. It tells how Pena had sent word to the workers from the cruiser to "Let the train go. We've made our point. Don't let others get hurt." How he and Valenta were somehow able to curb the cries for revenge back in the Union Hall that night. Some kind of strength and reason prevailed. Of course, headlines of "Rail Crossing Turned Battleground" spread around the nation. USX blamed the steelworkers as lawbreakers, and the Union blamed the police for brutality and the mayor for ignoring their warnings. And the mayor blamed the judge, who blamed the steelworkers for breaking his injunction.

In the days after, we all read and watched the news, as Valenta warned that "a time bomb" had been set, "And I cannot be responsible for what might occur." Then Mayor Olejko who feared "another Kent State," apologized to his friends Pena and Valenta declaring, "I'm a steelworker too. I begged them not to ship that steel." Finally in the *Journal* a steelworker asked the big question "Who is it that wants this violence?" Then he answered it himself, "Nobody but these bastards in Pittsburgh."

A thirty day, court injunction against any action by the company or the Union kept things quiet during December. I remember Marge saying, "Well, at least we'll have a sane Christmas." In January the workers all assembled in the old Palace Theatre and voted to accept the company's offer. It was over, but it wasn't.

Lying there in the hosptial watching the snow against the dark silhouette of the mill, I couldn't find sanity in any of it. Life was a lie and I was buried under its rock.

I was a victim of violence, had been violated, yet had no one to blame, so I blamed them all for years. Everything was rotten and spoiled for me, so I made a cripple of my spirit as well as my body. Hatred feeds no one, and for years I starved myself. I watched my brother Ted drift away from me as I turned to dope, trying to kill the pain and myself. I burned with loathing.

It's an old story, but it's mine. I struggled with it till it nearly took me down, but then something happened and I began to write of it, to tell its story. I began to make something from it and to write myself back.

You see, just before my mother died when I was at my worst, she gave me something. I had been living on the streets then, a prisoner to my despair. That Sunday morning I came into her kitchen without a word and picked up the newspaper. I looked at it while she was making me coffee; then I threw it on the floor and yelled, "This life is just shit, Mom. Just shit!" She looked at me, all dirty and tangled with pain, and I said, "Look! Look at me! Seeing is believing." I was that angry at everything.

I remember how Mom just walked over to me and brushed back my hair. She kissed my head and said, "I'm sorry that life has been so hard for you, Marco. You have so much to give, son." She just stood there breathing beside me, stroking back my long dirty hair and saying she loved me. It was too much her caring so, and something broke open in me. And as I cried against her soft dress, I knew how I had it all wrong. In her, believing was seeing, and she kept believing in me and seeing me more. I had been seeing the world through a funnel, and she turned it around and made it larger. We were all these fragments yet we each had the power to be part of the whole.

That's when I began to write again, when I could believe in it with her. Not long after that I met Maria standing on

Broadway watching the International Festival Parade honoring Lorain's returning hostage Terry Anderson. I remember, Maria looked up at me, a stranger, and said, "I guess we're all some kind of hostage." I knew then what a woman she was.

Maybe what Dr. Franco says is right, someday this story will be published and lots of people will read it. I'd like to do that for everyone. But it's already helped me. When I look around now, I see the life that's there in Ted and Marge or Mom and Dad, in their keeping family alive. It's in Esther and José and their fire for fairness and me and sweet Maria working things out together. I see it now in a young laughing Kenny or even Janis struggling towards herself, in Rudy and Carlos working their life, even Cassandra ruling the Deli. It's in Angelina writing her young girl's life in Lorain, Ohio, and in the old man in the blue coat gathering litter from around his building. In all of it is the sweet dignity of going on, of moving out from under the rock, even pushing it along. I know, because when I can write of it, it is enough.

IN THE SHADOWS OF STEELMILLS

Personal Narratives

BINGO AT THE MINGO SHOW

Like many of you, I am part of the "film generation" that grew up on a regular diet of movies and jujubes, popcorn and coke. Countless times in my Midwest youth, I walked out of the cool, quiet darkness of a movie house into the warm and noisy glare of my home town streets. Reality and the movies blurred. It is somewhat of an amazement now to see my hometown of Mingo Junction, Ohio, appear on the screen as an industrial backdrop for such films as *The Deer Hunter*, *Reckless*, and *Heart of Steel*. More than ever I recognize that reality and the movies merge somewhere in the heart of my past.

There was a time when I just about *lived* at the Mingo Show, soaking up the soft matinee light as the screen glowed with the real dreams of cowboys and show girls, gangsters and gun molls, comics and heroes, or the semi-sweet tales of Disney animals or loving families that touched and informed my life. Now we can all catch most of these old films on the American Movie Classics channel or colorized on Ted Turner's Network Television, or we can go out to the plaza and rent them for our home video cassette recorders. But you and I both know it won't be the same. The actors and story will be there, but the light from the television won't be as bright, and it won't reflect onto the warm upturned faces of the people of our hometown. Even at the mall multi-theaters today we seem to file in and out as strangers. But this is no lament over the cinemette world of wall-carpeted theatres; I have come to praise, not to blame, and to acknowledge what a real communal legacy we had in our hometown movie houses. For, more than our stadiums and gymnasiums, our churches and schools, our movie houses were our community fountains where we all met and drank a common culture.

Each small town had one as I discovered one day in 1970 while standing in the hardware store in Huron. I was looking around at the long layout of the building when someone explained it had once been the town movie house. Eating lunch at the Star Cafe in downtown Sandusky, I looked up from my chicken noodle soup to the ceiling and old projectionist window still open. The larger towns had several.

I know it was a mark of our independence when a group of friends could ride the bus (another cultural carrier) to Steubenville to share lunch and a first run film. There we could choose between The Capitol, The Grand, or the Paramount Theatres—even the names taught us something about style, as did the marbled urinals in the restroom, the dark ruby curtains, the white shirts and bow ties of the ushers. In the lush darkness we could all escape the glare and blare of our mill towns, try on the clothes of movie life, and return to our streets somehow wiser.

Fourteen cents was the ticket price for years at the Mingo Show, till they finally upped it to a dime and a nickel. So, we took back pop bottles, ran errands for neighbors, and went the movies often. On Friday and Saturday *High Noon* might be showing, and on Sunday, Monday, and Tuesday *The Quiet Man* would play. In the middle of the week, on Wednesday and Thursday, you could catch a showing of *A Streetcar Named Desire*. The lives on the screen seemed to extend our own as stretched into the fresh anguish of Marlon Brando or James Dean. We packed it in together at the OKAY Corral with Burt Lancaster and Kirk Douglas. For working class kids, we travelled a lot in our own hometowns.

Sometimes, if I had done my homework and if Grandma was going so that Mom had no sitter, I could go along for the midweek showing of a film like *Born Yesterday*. It would be dish and bingo night, and the lights would be on as the usher (some friend's older brother, or a kid who had graduated from his paper route) would hand us our gravy boats which Mom and Grandma would cradle on their laps beside me.

On bingo night after the first showing, the lights would come on. We could all suddenly see each other. The place would be packed with smiling neighbors and kids rubbing the sleep from their eyes. "Mingo Mike" Kendrach, the manager, would come out onto the stage with a couple of grinning ushers rolling in the bingo board and balls. He would tap the microphone a couple times and ask, "Is this on?" To which we would all shout back, "No, it's on!" and roar with laughter. Then he would smile and declare, "Good evening, everyone. And welcome to the Mingo Show." It seems now that the general response to this was a kind of relieved laughter. Then Mike would get serious as he announced, "Tonight, ladies and gentlemen, there will be fifty numbers called in our game. And I remind you that tonight's grand prize is . . ." (There was silence here, just to be certain we knew the stakes.) " . . . 200 dollars!" Real sighs went up at the sound of the amount, for most of us had already spent it in our heads buying new refrigerators and bikes. Of course, this was before our state lotteries made winning outrageous amounts seem almost common. "Yes, 200 dollars is tonight's prize," Mingo Mike would declare, and I could watch my mom holding her card as she smiled down on me, as if to say, "Boy, wouldn't your father be surprised."

I remember that a girl I liked in high school once won the jackpot amidst a cheering crowd. She got to go down front as they read off her card and pronounced her "Tonight's winner." She turned her $200 into a set of caps for her front teeth and became so famous that people would stop on the street just to point them out. "See her, she's the girl that won the Bingo jackpot at the show." Such downright glamour can be costly in a small town.

Mingo Mike would begin by reminding us to take the free space on our card (only those who paid adult prices received cards), and he would begin the reading of the balls handed to him by the smiling usher from a guest drawer. About 10 balls in he would caution us, "Remember, this is a *cover-all* game. All spaces must be covered in order to win." But we were still young into the game, and the odds seemed about right. Later, when he announced, "Ladies and gentlemen, we have only five numbers left," you could hear a bridge of sighs stretch across the audience—a sympathetic acceptance of our mutual fate.

Usually there were no grand winners, but always we each had won. We had shared the common experience of America—in the film and in each other. I carry lots of those old films within me—their human themes and gestures. I also still carry the warm faces of the people I lived with—my neighbors and friends, even my enemies and their moms, the folks from North Hill, Reservoir Hill, Church Hill, and the Bottom: the old women behind us who chattered in strange tongues—Slovak, Italian, Polish, Hungarian—their dark eyed daughters sitting with their mustached beaus, my black friends nested in the back corner, my English teacher and her best friend. Whether in a melting pot or rich salad bowl of American life, the experience made us all human and together. And as we piled out of the theatre into the evening light, people smiled into each other's eyes as they joked brightly about losing the grand prize—"And what would I do if I won—buy a new mink coat!" There was good cheer to spare. And as we walked out into the night, I would take the soft hands of my mother and grandmother and we would climb together the streets of home.

TO THE LANDFILL

The Volunteers of America rejected my mattress only minutes after I did. That morning, I took that fatal backward look, saw the sunken form of myself still there in and mattress, and heard myself exclaim, "I've been sleeping on *that? Enough!* Actually I realize now that my body must have been rejecting that mattress for years, only my sentiment had run interference with its message to my brain.

It was—believe it or not, after 20 years—our wedding mattress. Even Seally won't guarantee their posture-pedic beyond the fifteen year mark, and nobody will give you good odds on a marriage anymore. So my loyal heart probably blocked me from seeing and knowing about those spring marks, silver dollared circles indented along my spine.

My wife confessed little interest in making a change (about the mattress or her husband of years), said her half of the bed had been fine all these years. I knew then I'd have to live with the guilt and the expense of making the rejection—around $200 these days—and that's just for the mattress.

After flopping the old stained mattress onto the family room floor for a reckless day of bouncing and wrestling with the kids and napping with myself, I knew it had to make way for the new, had to be driven to the county landfill. Fresh home from work, my wife cried, "Just look at those spots! Do you want the world to see our life together?"

And so, this Monday morning I gather it up, into my arms (It actually folded)—drag it across the orange carpet (knocking over a dining room chair)—and burst through the front door—into the open glare of a neighbor lady who obviously believes I am dragging a body from the house. When she sees it is only a mattress, she indignantly turns away, leaving me to drag it across our damp grass and to stuff it whole into the mouth of our Volkswagen van.

While I am at it, I load up some tree trimmings, a box of assorted cans and plastic milk jugs, a cardboard box of crabgrass, a trash bag full of old wallpaper, and a pair of abandoned jogging shoes. Following some heavy breathing, a toweling down, and a quart of apple juice, I head towards the landfill—just a guy and his mattress.

On the way I must stop for lunch with a friend Tom at the town's only diner. Enjoying our talk of good films and our repast of fresh fish, I soon forget my burden in the van. When we emerge onto the parking lot, my friend nudges me, nods to the mattress inside the van and asks, "Out looking for girls, hey, Lar?"

Only the leaves dropping out of the side windows convinces him I am bound for the "dump" (my word for it). When I tell him I am rather fond of a monthly trip to the landfill (their word for it), he looks at me squarely and sighs, "Ah, so was I, old man, until about a month ago when I looked over the edge where I was dumping old clothes and found instead, a dead cow!"

"No!" I protest.

"But, yes! my friend, a dead cow being plowed into the earth along with the shingles and weeds and boxes of grass. I haven't been back since."

Now Tom is a filmmaker by profession, so I begin to suspect he has dreamed all this up from an old Salvador Dali or Monty Python film. In fact, I almost convince myself of it by the time I an driving across the tracks going out of town.

Denial is a wonderful thing, and just the opposite of nostalgia—a kind of out door for dreams where wishing can make it seem untrue. "What a kidder that guy is!" I like thinking.

However, by the time I drive through the gateway to the landfill I am not so sure anymore. At first the seagulls attract me—on a rainy day there are more of them here than along the lake. They have such a horrible screech...like the old ladies who used to yell at us when we'd run through their yards. "Eeek! Eeek! You kids, get out of there!"

Yet, I never know when to read a portent, never heed the warning while there is time. So, I pull up to the scales behind the read end of a garbage truck (Ever notice all the neat stuff those guys hang along the sides—salvaged toys and tools and only slightly destroyed junk?). From my position in line I can see into the sanitation barn where showers and brushes and clean suits line the walls—a regular clinic of sanitation—like a janitor's closet in a hospital. This prophylactic decompression chamber for the sanitation engineers somehow gives me the false assurance of science.

The fellow at the ticket booth is one of those big red-headed guys who always have their shirttail out and sport a rugged smile. He is writing me up when I think to ask about the dead cow story. "Say, a friend of mine said that the last time he was here there was a dead cow thrown in with the trash." Grinning to show I'm not a complete fool, then waiting like one, I finally ask, "Could that be true...I mean..."

I am about to shake off this outrage completely when I hear: "Oh, yeah." Stepping up to my window, he exclaims, "We get your cows and hogs and chickens in here. Oh, yeah, trucks of them."

"Well, what do you know," I try to shut him up, would like to pull away, but he still holds my ticket. Somehow the idea of a stray cow had become barely tolerable, but the image of a whole herd of animals from Old MacDonald's farm lying around in the muck brings on a wave of nausea that blends perfectly with the sweet odor of decay I am busy ignoring. "I'll be damned," I try to say with a grin.

"Oh, year, and we get your cats and dogs all the time. I'll tell you..." His face serious with fact, "We've had whole ponies and horses brought in here."

"Horses!" leaps from my lips, and I pop the clutch. Quickly I start it again as he leans in the window. "And once...from Jungle Jerry's Safari Show...we had ourselves a *dead baby elephant* right here at the landfill!"

By this time I am roaring away sliding in he gravel and trying to close my window. I know nobody obeys the 10 mph speed limit, but I'm not even trying. I'm not sure whether he is shouting for me to slow down or continuing his list of dead creatures, but I know he looks like some kind of red haired caveman as he waves his arms in my rearview mirror.

To tell the truth, I'm uncertain why I'm telling you all this, or what it all mean. Maybe confession is another form of denial. Maybe my making a story of it helps me to put it away in some kind of memory shoebox with my other receipts. I do know that day, I tumbled the soft fossil of my mattress bravely over the edge, watching it flop over itself then slide down, placing a large dream cushion between me and the creatures below.

THE COMPANY OF WIDOWS

Every couple of months or so I return to the industrial Ohio Valley with its deep green Appalachian walls along that big winding river. And lately as I come into town bouncing over the gaping potholes of Steubenville streets, stopping at the traffic light beside that huge bridge to West Virginia, I stare at the new monument to the steel valley, a statue of a laborer in shiny asbestos suit frozen at that moment when he taps a sample from the blast furnace floor. He seems intent upon his job, only there is no blast furnace floor, just this laborer alone in time and space. I admire the statue's simple directness, its human scale and respect for reality. For me, this whole steel valley remains as real and fluid as the hot flowing iron of memory.

As I round the curve under the Market Street Bridge, my windows down to make a summer breeze, there is that aftertaste of something burnt in the air, and I swear you can taste it too in the water, as bittersweet as rust. Heavy barges of coal and ore move down river beside me as the gray air billows from smokestacks, rises and crests in a dark heavy cloud. I am enough of an outsider now to notice this; insiders never do, or if it gets too heavy and they are forced to cough each time they speak, they blame it on the milltown across the river—"Smells like Follansbee!" This place so marked by extremes of beauty and waste, is my place, my hometown, my family—and I breathe and swallow it again.

"It ain't all bad," as they say, and I look over to see my wife awake now as we come into "Mingo Town." She smiles too at being home, and we wake our twelve year old daughter, who asks, "Are we at Grandma's yet?" I smile as the car winds up the steep hill, and pulls in before a yellow brick home. I unload our bags and leave the women here at Ann's mothers, then drive down St. Clair hill, staring into the steaming cauldrons of the mill. At Murdock Street I turn right, coast downhill, and pull in behind my mother's car. She has taken down the front maple, leafless for years, so that the whole place looks a little different and a whole lot the same; a three story wooden frame house with worn green shingles along the edge of Ohio Route 7.

Mrs. Maul nods to me as I get out—neighbors still, her yard still cared for like her retarded son who is now 33 and staring out the widow at me. I wave then note how Mom's porch needs the mill dirt squirted off. I take the broom by the door, and start dancing it across the green painted concrete till she hears me, comes to the front window laughing, "Get in here, you nut."

It is at least a five minute wait as she wrestles her door locks, three of them where once there were none. But I don't object, I want her safe, and with the recent break-ins and thefts from cars, I tell her I will install another if she wants. "Don't worry," she says hugging me home, "We old girls keep an eye out for each other."

In Mom's house one never gets further than the "television room" where the set is always on. I've found her sleeping here some nights in her reclining chair in the glow of a snowy screen. We sit and she gives me news of who has died or been arrested, and word of my lost siblings; she offers me candy and a glass of root beer. She is sixty-four this year, my father's fatal heart attack upstairs, now three years past. Though we often speak of him, of what he'd think, of how he used to work so hard, of his joking with the kids, we never address his death. We both know that he is gone—the whole house echoes his absence—but we won't recall for each other those weeks around his death when we went through his things, sorting out tools and clothes, taking papers from the mill to the social security office in Steubenville. It still breaks my heart remembering my mother sitting in that office, hearing her say to the stranger, "My husband's dead, now what do I do?"

Only this time as she brings in a plate of store-bought cookies, I am surprised to hear her say, "That day your dad died, he took a handful of these and a glass of milk. I remember, he said he was just going upstairs to lie down. He said he had to rest."

I cannot breathe for the weight of this, something caught in my own chest which somehow asks, "Mom, what happened that day Dad died? Who found him, did you?"

Our eyes just touch before she goes to sit, "Oh, yes, it was me that found him—there in our bed—asleep I thought at first, yet somehow I knew." She takes a breath as the scene begins, "He'd come home from golfing with his buddies saying that his arm was hurting. He started golfing several times a week since the mill retired him." Her eyes look distant as she talks, like she's watching all this on a television screen somewhere. "I called to him, touched his arm, and he felt cold lying there. God I was scared, so I called Darlene and she called the emergency squad. They got here quick. His friend Brownie was with them. He's the one came downstairs to tell me, 'Jeanny,' he said, 'there's nothing more we can do.' I remember him standing right here where you are, saying that. 'There's nothing more we can do,'" and she sighs. "Brownie's a good old boy, been your father's friend since they were school boys."

"Was there a doctor who came?" I have to ask.

"No, just the paramedics, but then they took him straight to the hospital where he was pronounced dead." Suddenly she looks at me as though she has awakened out of a trance and is waiting for me to explain. Only I can't. All I can say is, "It must have been hard for you. I'm sorry I wasn't around." There is a silence between us so still that we notice the hoot and crash of the mill as the trains take a haul of slag down to the pits. The mill is always there in this town—in the sounds and smells, the color of the air and in the talk—"What they got you workin', midnight?" "We'd come up, but Michael's workin' four-to-twelve next month...." Work is the fabric of life here.

Married at eighteen, my father worked as a brakeman on the railroad at Weirton Steel for forty years, till they forced him to retire. All this is *there* inside the room—this awareness of a life.

"How'd you get through it all, Mom?"

"Well, Darlene was here, and your sister Debbie had come down by then. I think Dr. Ruksha came by and gave me something. I can't remember now. Debbie would."

There's another long silence as we think about all that's just been said. This is further than we've ever gone into it, the gritty details of a death, and it's almost asthough we've stirred up a part of ourselves we thought was dead. I smile at her, "How come we never talked about this, Mom?"

She looks back, "I don't know." And then she thinks to say, "I know he's gone—Lord how I miss that old boy—but he's still here inside this house. You know, I can feel him sometimes. I think I hear him calling up from the basement, 'Honey, where's my work clothes?' or some such thing. I almost answer him, then I stop." She smiles quietly, "I guess I'm losing touch. But you know, I always feel better when I think of him, like having him back in a dream."

I go over and hug her in her chair, and we can both sense the grief in each other. "What does it all mean?" she sighs, and I just hold her, so frail and quiet.

"You did all you could, Mom. All anyone can."

Now it is I who have to move about, so I walk out into the kitchen for a drink. The radio is playing the area talk show—'Will the schools be forced to consolidate if the mills don't pay back taxes?' It is a mix of local gossip and preparing for the worst. My wife's uncle talks of retiring at forty-five. "What do I care?" he asks, "I can't let the mills decide my life. What's going to happen anyway, when it all shuts down? Have you thought of that?" And he shakes his head sitting on his front porch, "Who owns these mills? Who decides what happens here?" I shake my own head. "We steelmakers are a forgotten race," he concludes and I have no more answer for him than for my mother in the other room.

I could tell her of my own dreams of my father—of how he appeared in our house, smiling and tried to tell me a joke I couldn't get—how he laughed as if to say he was okay now. I know I felt good for a week, but dreams fade quicker than memories. Back in this valley the struggle toughens you or it breaks your heart. And where do you draw the line?

I think of how my father didn't complain of his arm or chest on the day he died, and I wonder if he might not be alive if he had. But, wasn't he trained here not to feel the pain, not to complain? Pouring my coffee, measuring my cream, I wonder how much we give up to survive? How much did my father?

I stir it together and know these are futile questions, yet somewhere I've learned that ignoring a truth creates another sort of pain and a kind of blind numbness around the heart. I remember how Dad, scout master of my youth, would stop our car on the street to break up a kids' fight; he couldn't let a wrong go on. His working so hard, sending two boys through college, may have been his own way of rebelling against a silent lie. I take a drink of valley coffee and sit back down on the couch.

While my mother goes to take her medication I leaf through the local *Herald Star*. When she returns I ask, "Mom, what's this parade they're having uptown in Steubenville today—a Festival Homecoming? Do you want to go?"

She smiles, "Sure, when is it?" Like a child now she welcomes small adventures and a chance for company. I know that kitchen radio is her best friend most days, that's why I bought it for her, and to quell my own guilt for moving away to my quiet home along the lake.

"They say at 2:00, but there's already a street fair on Fourth and Market if you want to take that in. Have you seen it?"

"Debbie and Michael took Robin the other night," as she sits. "They said she rode a pony in the street. I can't imagine that. A pony in the middle of Market Street that used to be so busy with traffic."

"Yeah," I say, and we both know the story of how the old downtown of Steubenville died four years ago after the layoffs, then again with the opening of the Fort Steuben Shopping Mall. And we both secretly wish we could be wrong about this, that the town will yet survive. Somehow our valley toughness doesn't exclude a capacity to dream.

*   *   *

At noon I show up again having retrieved my wife and daughter. My mother-in-law Sue has joined us in this summer thirst for a celebration. A widow like Mom, Sue carries her John with her all the time. Instead of wearing a widow's black, she refused to smile for a year and a half. She's a strong Italian woman whose fierce integrity and hard work make her a legend in her neighborhood. John too did his 40 years in the mills, as a millwright—humble and happy on his job till they took it from him claiming his eyes were weak. They were weak but twice as strong as the benefits the mill paid for his "early out." I know these forced retirements didn't kill our dads, but I curse the thoughtless pain they brought to good people. Sue works now in the school cafeteria—baking cookies and cakes, fish and french fries for a troop of teenagers. They give her a hard time but love her cooking. They always ask whether she cooked it before they buy...she is seventy.

My wife Ann and daughter Suzanne are like her in their strong will. In the Valley you learn early, if you learn at all, that work and self-belief are your strongest tools. My mother-in-law's favorite saying, besides "The rich get richer, and the poor get poorer" and "At least we *eat* good," is ... "Well, we have each other."

Ann offers the front seat to my mother, but she refuses, climbing into the back—"No, no, we belong back here. Don't we, Sue? The merry widows—and Suzanne." We all laugh, and they begin to talk as I cruise up river to the celebration, to the hope a parade brings. As we enter town from the North I search for a parking place—up close and free. I must prove to all these women that they haven't a fool for a son, husband or father.

Finally, we pull onto the hot asphalt of the city lot, and I feed dimes to the meter. We cross the light down Adams to the street fair. The parade will follow these outside streets and march a square around the intersection of Fourth and Market. It's a good thing too, as those two streets are packed with noisy citizens barking back at the game keepers, standing in line for rides, or wolfing down Italian sausage and onions with a sudsy Budweiser in the afternoon. The whole street smells like a local bar, and there is hardly room to pass as we bump good naturedly into our neighbors. A flow in this human river, pushed on, I almost lose my wife who waves a hand above the heads. We laugh on the street corner, "So many people," I say, and she adds, "And we actually know some of them," an inside joke to small-town emigrants living in anonymous suburbs where the faces seem familiar yet you know none of them.

As a rock band blasts and rumbles from the flatbed of a truck, we feel at "home." And though we know this busy downtown street will become a deserted crime area again come Monday, for a while, our memory is washed by the flood of our senses.

Sue tells Ann to tell me that it's time to find a place to watch the parade, and so I look around then lead us back from Washington Street, only this time along the sidewalk, past the back of the Italian and Irish booths smelling of spaghetti and cornbeef with nearly matching flags, past the abandoned J.C.Penney's building, the closed furniture and clothing stores—so empty and dark inside—past the Slovak church's perogi and raffle booth, to the corner of Fourth and Adams.

The old Capital Theatre has been leveled to build a store to sell tires and auto parts. It's been gone for years, but each time it hits me with its large sense of absence. In fact I realize that I have been vibrating with this same sense of presence and absence since we arrived. Struck by the sense of what is here and what is not, I struggle to assimilate—the change.

In the midst of parents pushing their children toward a noisy, street merry-go-round, I recall how my wife and I once sat close together in the cushioned seats of the Capital Theatre while Tony and Maria of *West Side Story* sang so desperately of their love struggle. It was the first time we kissed. Perhaps my whole little family really began in search of such close moments? Perhaps. What I do know is that things change, even in the old town. Facing that, I know my real problem is understanding the direction of that change.

Waiting here on the curb along the corner, I've been noticing things. Not just the noise and vacant stores but the changed sense of the place. What has survived and how? The angry fumes of the One-Hour Dry Cleaners still spill out onto the street, and I remember its sickening smell and sticky feel as I picked up a suit, standing there forced to breath it as I watched the weary movement of the women at their mangles, caught the hurried tone of the clerks. And of course the bars are still here, one for every third storefront, and the Sports & Cigar places not driven out by the legal lottery. One bakery is still open, reminding me of time spent waiting for the bus breathing the hearty bread and donut smells till I had to purchase "Just one, please" from the Downtown Bakery. All the Five and Dime stores have been converted to self-serve drugstores, the restaurants to offices or video rentals, the clothing stores empty as night.

I stand there making this mental documentary when my daughter insists, "Dad, I'm hungry." We adults suddenly look to each other and realize she is right, we have forgotten lunch. I look back to the booths, then down Adams and smile, one of the brightest moments of the day, for we are a half block away from one of the best pizza shops in Ohio, perhaps the world.

"I'll be right back," I tell them, and take my daughter's hand to lead her down the street to DiCarlo's Italian Pizza. Inside, the mixed aromas of parmesian—warm dough— spicey pepperoni and sauce bring me back. It is a Roman pizza they make, sold by the square, and the crust is crisp yet chewy with juicy chunks of tomato melting into the mozarella cheese and pepperoni which they throw on last likescattered seed. I point this out to my child, all the while remembering those years of standing at this same counter watching the rich ritual of the men tossing dough hard on counters, of their moving the pizza up the oven drawers as it rose steadily to a climax—cut and boxed, a rubber band snapped around the corners, the holes popped to keep it crisp. We buy two dozen and hurry back to our crowd, to that first bite into the steaming slab, chewing it well, a piece at a time. And it's good to taste how some things stay the same.

Standing as we eat, I notice the need for napkins, to catch the dripping but also to keep it clean from all the street dirt blowing along the curb. "It's a shame," Sue clucks, nodding to the way litter lies along the street—not just cigarette butts, though there are plenty of those, but whole bags from Burger King, empty pop and beer cans that the residents step over, like hard stones on the sidewalk. "The city levy didn't pass," I am told, and I nod as if I understand, but it is all wrong. Like watching your child pulled from a sports game, I am really torn that what seems so precious to me feels so easily abused. Yet I check my sense of righteousness knowing how much I've moved away from here, to my suburban life, a college teaching job, a safe haven along Lake Erie. I do not wish to accent my estrangement. I eat my pizza.

People begin lining the curbs standing or seated in their lawn chairs. They stand and talk or occasionally watch up the street for the start of things. The police walk by us, a kid waits then darts across the street. Something is about to begin. Watching the faces of people standing near me I look for the familiar but find only the strange...a woman in a POISON T-shirt yanking her child up by the arm—smacking her really hard on the butt, screaming "I told you to pee before we left!" this time a smack to the face, "Didn`t I?" No one says anything. "Well, didn't I?" The child only wails while the mother bellows, "Now, you run home and change those pants. You'll miss the parade." The straw haired woman seems oblivious to all around her, as though the street is her home. This is something our parents and neighbors never did, no dirty laundry aired in the street.

Her husband joins her now on stage—and yes, he is a hairy guy with those dark blue tattoos flaming up and down his arms. He brushes by her. "Hey, babe, I'm goin' for a beer!" falls off his lips like spit, as he pushes his way through the crowd.

"Oh, no you're not!" she shouts at him. "You're not leaving me again with *these kids!*" And it seems her whole life is a series of exclamations as she walks off leaving her children at our feet. They don't seem to notice, and most of the crowd looks back up the street trained now at ignoring these little unforgivable scenes of communal violence. It is my mother-in-law who hisses, "*Sceev-o*" and folds her pizza away in her napkin. It's an Italian expression, a succinct verb that means, "It makes me sick," and I know it is not the pizza but the mean ugliness that has repulsed her. It haunts the streets as I look hard at the faces in the crowd of locals who seem as strangely foreign to me as the news from Iraq. It's like watching the films made in this area—Robert DeNiro's "The Deer Hunter," or Peter Strauss's "Heart of Steel." The setting is right but the people are all wrong—not because they are actors but because they are portraying the valley and its people at their most desperate to preach Hollywood despair or false hope. That film life feels close yet alien to anyone who knows this place, a twin hurt that confuses me like these wounded faces around me. They are not the faces I grew up with here who lived well though poor, and shared the good that they had and were.

As I watch this woman turn back I try to guess her age, but it is impossible—the facial lines and glassy eyes, yet her young children at our feet. She turns to us, motions to her kids, yells to my puzzled mother, "I'll be right back!" And so we find ourselves baby-sitting her girls on the street corner. They take no notice until we offer them a pizza which they grab and gobble down, thanking us only with their eyes. It's an awkward scene, but this human gesture seems the only way to dispel the curse of this family's life.

"Who are these people, Mom?" I hear myself asking.

"Oh, I don't know her," she says, then realizes what I've asked. "There's a new crowd that lives downtown now."

"Where did they come from?"

Sue answers, "When everyone started moving out of downtown, they started moving in." She gestures broadly to the old buildings across the street, and I see above the storefronts the backs of buildings—windows with ragged curtains, bags of trash out in the street beside junked cars. And my heart sags like the dirty clouds or this child's heavy diaper.

"Apartments are cheap now, cause nobody wants to live where so many muggings go on." Sue goes on to report the worst and most recent incidents while I wonder which came first—the crime or the abandonment. She can't help telling these stories, because it has happened to her friends; it's a part of her life now. She plays out her old storyteller's hand—hoping in telling it to somehow understand.

And I think of another conversation last week with a city planner now working as a car salesman. "No jobs for city planners," he jokes. So when I tell him of my dismay at understanding the way cities change, he describes for me the 'myth of urban renewal.' "See, they throw up a few new office buildings that look good to the outsiders. Right?" I remember nodding. "Only what you don't see is also what you get. To the city poor it means something else—less and worse housing. Where do you think all the 'homeless' people come from?" he asks while downing a half cup of coffee. "I'll tell you. Urban renewal drives some of them into the street and it drives a lot of others away—to smaller cities like your hometown where they have no sense of past and no hope of a future. And so there they live *unconnected*, just using up the present."

I had nothing more to say then nor now, as this parade begins. I just stand here thinking: of the fathers who worked this valley farming labor into families along the river land, and of the widows now forced to watch the rich soil used up, spoiled by greed and unconcern. I know that my father had no answer for this either, and for once I am glad he doesn't have to be here to watch it all happen. I just stare across the street at an older man tending cars in the parking lot. He moves aimlessly from car to car, checking tags, and I recognize something in his face. My mother whispers his name—a classmate of mine—his face a shadow of my own.

Held there on the curb of the Steubenville street that feels so close yet strange, I become my own mute statue.

As the parade goes by, I watch how the faces light up at so little. The children are smiling at a clown squirting water from his motorcycle. A float of Junior Women toss candy at our feet. My mother waves to friends. I find myself nodding to everyone, yet inside myself I am thinking of the five words given to me by my ex-city planner: "Abandonment creates its own culture." It sums up my own confused pain now, and I say it over and over to myself, "Abandonment creates its own culture." In the summer heat the parade passes, we smile into late afternoon sun, and then we take the widows home.

RIVER OF STEEL

Stories

"And who is it you could not love
once you've heard their story?"
-Pax Christi

HOME CASUALTIES

In 1942 most of the young men of my generation were off to war in Europe or the Far East. My brother Bill was in the Philippines, while I was left on the homefront making steel at the Weirton plant. You see, one cold October day during football season my collar bone was broken in a practice drill. I heard it crack inside of myself, and I knew. Then, when they came to set it, they did something wrong so that I was left with a right arm that looks like a road map of varicose veins. "Break one of those, Roy, and you're a dead man," old Doctor Albright said, smiling, then he looked away. That was all that was ever said about it, till I went in for my draft notice.

So I spent the war in the steel mills, where they needed strong backs and arms as tools for making weapons at home, and where the doctors didn't care to look that close at veins.

Sarah didn't mind my injury, was overjoyed in fact when I told her I wouldn't be going. "You'll be home safe with me," she said, "And...you can take me to all the school dances," she smiled. I'll tell you, I couldn't hardly understand it myself let alone explain to her the hurt of once more being cut from the team. That next year Sarah and I ran off and got married in Paris, Pennsylvania. Sarah was already pregnant with Paul.

We spent our honeymoon driving around Pittsburgh in my brother's Dodge. We rode the cable car up North Hills and ate in a little Chinese restaurant downtown. That night we slept at the State Line Motel outside of Weirton. We didn't even pack a suitcase. Sarah cried when she saw there wasn't any hot water, but we warmed up good in that little bed. Once in the night I week and watched her sleeping, then fell asleep counting trucks cruising by on old Route 22. I wasn't a failure that night.

Next day we drove up to Sarah's folks' place over on Wilson Avenue in Steubenville. We could tell her pap was home, 'cause the Packard was parked outside. I remember him sitting on the front porch swing puffing on his pipe, then spitting in an old Maxwell House Coffee can. "Well, you better treat her right, boy, or I'll break that arm and neck of yours for good." Then he smiled a little and got us a beer. Oh yeah, Sarah's mother locked herself in the bathroom overnight.

All I remember about telling my folks is we sat down at the kitchen table and drank coffee. My father asked two questions, was Sarah pregnant and when did I start in the mill. I moved Sarah's stuff into my bedroom. Mom fixed a chicken dinner that Sunday evening, and we all listened to the radio till 8:00 o'clock. I remember hearing the footsteps down the hallway as Sarah crept in beside me, and I thought about how my own folks must have started once like us.

Paul was born in '42 and we were living in the mill apartments up on Wheeler Street by then. He had his mother's clear blue eyes, but the Metzger's way of looking deep into you. Sarah took sick for a couple months before and right after, so Mom would walk over to our place and take care of both her and the baby when I had to work. I'd be going out the back door while she was starting in the kitchen. I tried to thank her once, and she just looked up from the dishes, "Lord knows, son, we're your family." I wished someone had told that to Sarah's mom. And at night when I'd come home, Mom would be sleeping in the living room with her stockings unrolled and her shoebox of tax stamps at her feet. I wasn't no failure to them, just a son.

From the backporch fire escape of the Wheeler apartments you could see the whole Ohio Valley—green hills and long river, with the mill plant spread out like a field of factory, rolling out steel sheets for the hulls of warships. The ships were being built some place in New Jersey, so we never got to see them, but they had their pictures posted about the mill so we could see "Our part in the big war effort."

It seemed like everything had a quiet to it back then, like we were all doing what we could, waiting about and listening for the war news of our troops over. At night during the Big Bands Parade, the announcer who introduced the singers for the Dorsey band would come on in a clear but emotional voice and announce the victories and the losses in Germany, Italy, and the Philippines. It was like hearing the ball scores from your hometown, over there. Life seemed both distant and close then, caught in a sort of slow motion till we watched it flash on the newsreel at the movies.

It was pretty quiet all around, as we all dug in for the duration, and planted our home gardens. Of course, there was rationing—butter, rubber, gasoline—but we weren't going anywhere anyway. Sharing in the struggle helped me not notice the looks I'd get sometimes at the grocery on in the movie line asking with their eyes why I wasn't "over there" with my buddies. Then slowly, one by one, the casualties started coming home—not the death notices but the men themselves who crept back into town without limbs or wounded about the face and eyes. You'd run into then at Whitey's Poolroom or on the sidewalk someplace, and they'd look at you and turn away like they needed glasses and wouldn't get them. I think they knew it was really us who couldn't see.

That same year my wife's younger brother Dick died of rheumatic heart, our first home casualty. Sarah cried night after night like something sweet had been lost to her, like one heart had broken another. She couldn't talk about it then, so most nights I'd sit out on the porch alone reading the paper and listening to the radio against the roar and hoot of the mill. About a month later her folks asked us over to Sunday dinner for the first time. We showed up about noon and Sarah went in to help her mother while I sat on the front porch talking mill talk with her pap—production and all. Sarah's mother was still taking Dick's death pretty hard though, so mostly we ate in silence. Then she pipes up with, "Sarah, you and he may take home a can of that coffee and some preserves when you go." It was almost getting friendly. After desert her mom got up all of a sudden and went crying into the bathroom. Sarah got real quiet herself, so her pap and I tried to keep things going by talking sports.

Later, we were all three standing around the front-door with her mom up the stairs still locked inside. "Mr. Cochran," I said, "we sure appreciate the chicken dinner. Please tell your wife." I meant it too, even though the food was served without seasoning, like her pap's hard way of grieving without tears.

"Daddy, Roy and I want you and Mother to come visit us next Sunday," Sarah spoke it like we'd planned, then turned her head to her handkerchief. I was waiting for him to take and hug her, and I guess I'd be waiting there still, 'cause this red faced Irishman had already said his piece by handing us the coffee can. So I took it and patted Joe lightly on the arm, "Sorry about your boy, Joe," I started, but Sarah nodded me off.

Walking down the street under summer streetlights we could hear the steady roar of the mill, and I could feel my wife's poor heart pacing like a pet rabbit. We passed the slow maples, sliding our way home, and for some fool reason I started to sing, "I'll be down to get you in a taxi, Honey." I sang it all the way home.

Oh yeah, one Sunday that summer her pap and I went to see a ballgame together. We loaded up on fresh peanuts at a place near the Fenway ballpark. He'd been going to the Pirate's opener for as along as he could remember. Yet this year something was missing from the ballgame, something just wasn't there for him. In the majors that year they hardly had enough players and lots of those who did had to get special permission to leave their defense jobs just to play. I heard they even thought about cancelling the season or at least doing away with the night games. But, like us, they found a way to keep things going. A lot of older players even got called back.

I was beginning to enjoy it all, the color of the field, the players' uniforms and their ways of doing little things like tipping their caps, tapping their bat against their spikes. Then Mr. Cochran started in yelling at the players. Each time some fielder made an error, he'd get all red faced and start cursing. Then maybe he'd spit at our feet and say, "Ah, it ain't the same. It ain't the same." And when the first baseman had the ball trapped in his mitt and couldn't find it, old Joe stood up so quick, and I thought he was having a heart attack or stroking on a peanut shell, 'cause he didn't say anything, just turned and grabbed his coat, jerked with his head to motion me that we were going, then stepped right on his pile of peanut shells. We were almost out of the stdium as the organ started playing "Take Me Out to the Ballgame," for the seventh inning stretch.

About when we reached the West Virginia border, he looked over at me then back at the road. "Damn this war," he said to himself, but I heard it clear as day.

The next year, '43, our little Leroy was born. We wanted to name him Dick, after Sarah's brother, but her mother wouldn't have it. "Never mind," I told Sarah. That night in bed, I said, "Sarah, here we are in our little apartment with two boys and both of us not yet twenty. We sure must be crazy in love." She was quiet a moment, then started laughing and we got to loving after that.

Most Sundays we'd have dinner with my folks and read the latest letter from brother Bill in the Philippines, or from my sister Mary off working in the Pentagon. Mom kept the house going all by herself, and I do think the only time I ever say her without an apron was Sundays at church. She never complained and always said we each had to play our part.

In the evening, if Sarah was up to it and the boys were tucked away early, we'd sing with the radio on the front porch. Our favorite tune then was "Prisoner of Love" by the guy, Perry Como. They played it a lot on KDKA. "Alone from night to night you'll find me, / too weak to break the chairs that bind me. / I need no shackles to remind me, / I'm just a prisoner of love." Sarah would be sitting in her best shirt-waist dress with her hair pulled back in the warm night air. The mill sounds were drowned in melody.

"Roy, honey, do you ever feel that way, like you're stuck here with me and the boys?"

She'd surprise me like that some times, and I wouldn't have an answer at first. So I'd just speak the truth. "You know, there's something I like so much about that song and I can't explain it. But it ain't the words. It's more the sound of the music in his voice. Do you know what I'm saying? The sound of going on."

She looked right into my eyes and I could see that evening sky in hers. I just wanted to hold her till the whole

war was over. Then I said, "It's how I feel about life sometimes, like I feel all this music but the words just don't make
any sense."

Then we'd just look at each other across the quiet, and
pretty soon sneak up to our room, neither of us prisoners.

The next year we got our first car about the time my
pop came to work with me on the railroad at Weirton Steel.

The car was an old model-A that I worked on down
at Ernie's Garage. I used to work for Ernie in high school. So
when he hauled in the Ford, he rang me up and sold it to me
for his hauling costs plus fifty bucks. I never did get all the
dents out of the body, and the tires had more patches than the
Hindenburg, but the engine ran and ran on that car. I was
afraid to take it to work 'cause the mill dirt would ruin what
finish it had left, so I still took the bus most days. Maybe the
bus took forever, but it was like nobody was in such a big
hurry back then, and I'd unwind on the way home or as I
climbed the hill in the dusky dark. I knew each slab of
sidewalk, each house and yard up that hill, each step one
closer to Sarah and the boys.

I have to tell you, once Sarah packed root beer in my
thermos, 'cause she knew it was my favorite. When it ex-
ploded, I was sitting in the last seat on the bus and didn't say
a thing till the others followed the puddle back to my legs;
then there wasn't much I could say. I remember hurrying
home to tell Sarah that night, so we could have a good laugh,
but she just ran into the bedroom and threw herself across the
bed with the ironing. When she cane back into the kitchen I
handed her the cup of coffee I made, and we just started
laughing till we woke the babies.

Sarah was always wanting to take a ride in our little
car. She'd pack up the boys and a lunch on a Saturday, and

we'd head over the Ohio hills, down past Bloomingdale onto the county roads. I'd be driving along with her quiet at my side, the boys sleeping on the back seat. Sarah never spoke what she really felt then, 'cause I think her she never really knew, but somehow her face would get quiet while her eyes deepened, needing or dreaming something she couldn't ever say, but I knew she loved me.

Pop lost his job at Wheeling Steel about this time 'cause he wouldn't follow the new orders. He was a mill brakeman too, like me, his whole life. And when the orders came down to do away with the fireman on the engine, he wouldn't obey. "It just isn't safe," he'd say. "It isn't right." He was a union man and wouldn't break the code, but then the union went and broke it themselves. So when he refused to work without a fireman, he didn't even have the union to back him. They all just let him go that summer of '43.

I'd go over home and find him working in the garden, which was really huge that year. He even built a chicken coop and a new garage at the end of the yard, but I could see they were using up their savings quicker than chicken feed.

"Dad, I think I can get you in at Weirton Steel, if you're willing." He was reading the paper on the backporch steps. Then he folded the paper over his lap and looked me over like I was a preacher or something. I don't think he really knew what to do with his life. He'd given every job he ever did his best and knew no other way.

"What's the deal over there?" he spoke low. "They still got the firemen on the engines, or no?" The night was setting shadows about the big features of his face.

"We don't have no firemen, Dad, but then we don't have a union to go against over there."

"What you got then?" I could see he really wanted to understand.

"We got an 'agreement.' It says the owners will match whatever the other steelworkers get, but we don't have to go on strike." He looked down at his Sunday shoes and began to shake his head.

"I know how you feel about fair labor, Dad. You been union all your life, but where was that union when you needed them at Wheeling Steel?"

Suddenly he slapped his paper down on the sidewalk like it was a fly he swatted, but it wasn't, 'cause he turned and looked at me in a way that really hurt, like I was maybe the fly he'd like to swat. "Boy, it ain't the unions I been loyal to all these years. It's the truth of what's fair. Haven't you learned that yet!"

I felt awful sitting there causing more hurt. I turned to go, then turned back to speak, "Dad, I know all that, and I'm sorry for what I just said. I just know you'd feel better bringing home that old paycheck again."

A long dark silence settled on that porch, so that I could feel his face looking at mine. Then he rose and walked past me into the house. The night closed around me on that lonely porch, and still I had the long walk home.

On Wednesday Dad called to say he'd take the job if I could arrange it. By Friday he was starting as a new brakeman on engine #11, the blast furnace crew.

That next week I ran into him several times in the locker room in the mornings. "How's everything going, Dad?" I'd ask and stand there waiting while he laced up his shoes.

"Just fine, boy," he's say, now raising his head. Then I'd walk away.

When I asked Carmony's crew how Dad was doing, someone grinned and yelled from the engine cab, "The old man's doing just fine, Roy!"

You see, there was this distance then that could come up sudden between people, even people you loved, and maybe especially them. Yet we all knew we were into something big—that and love held us, but it was often an uneasy wait, like sitting outside a hospital room, and we all knew that some of the real wounds would never show, not even on x-rays.

Anyway, on the following Friday I was sitting on the locker room steps eating my lunch. I remember holding two hard boiled eggs in one hand while I searched with the other for some salt in the lunchbox. Bob McKenzie came around the corner of the building and stopped quick, "Roy!" he said without a breath. "Listen, you better come quick, 'cause your old man's been hurt down on furnace three."

I remember standing there and crushing those two eggs in my hand without a thought, then dropping them into my lunchpail. We took off walking as fast as we could down the blast furnace alley. Railroaders are superstitious about the dangers of their work, so I wasn't surprised when Bob disappeared before I got to the slag cars, shut down beside the spill.

"What happened—where's my dad?" my heart spoke these words pounding louder than any furnace. The slag spill was a mass of steaming rock beside the track, so that at first only the furnace crew appeared above.

"They took the old man into the yard office, over there," someone yelled and pointed with a shovel.

Inside, a ring of men stood around his body stretched out upon the desk. I closed the door and stepped into the hush of whispers going round.

"Roy," it was the engineer, Howard Terelli. "Your dad, he's pretty bad, got caught between the engine and the first car. He was trying to make a coupling to get the other cars away from the spill."

Tarelli's small shoulders kept shaking as he talked. "I couldn't see out the fireman's side, and I kept backing up. I swear there was nothing I could do."

"It's okay, Howard," I said, easing him down onto a bench beside the water cooler.

Then I saw Dad. He was all broken and torn, lying there on top of all those damn papers. His eyes kept rolling toward the window light. While we waited for the emergency wagon, I tried to make him know who I was. His body was shaking so that I put my arm under his head and held it on my knee. "It's alright, son," he said, "It's all a man can do..." and I tried to say then that I knew because I really did, but I don't think he heard me.

He was already getting cold when we reached the hospital and they took him. I remember sitting outside the hospital steps for almost an hour, string down that long valley of river and smoke. You could smell it even up there. I remember how I felt like I wasn't even there for awhile. I just kept staring down that valley till it felt like something was gone forever and something else was here. Then Sarah and her pap drove up and took me home in the Packard.

It was ruled an "accidental death." Without a union, the mill settled our claim out of court—for $1,300. But it ain't worth the bitterness. This ain't about that. Dad was buried in the hills near his home around Richmond and we moved in with Mom until my brother Bill and my sister Mary and the other veterans all came marching home.

WOMAN VOICES

ONE

My brother was always breaking his glasses. Sometimes we'd be sitting at table eating and someone would notice his face turning red and his eyes squeezing shut. He was twisting his glasses till they'd break. Sometimes he'd start banging them on the table before we could get to him. And sometimes at night when he was roaming around our house, he would break our glasses. And none of us could see well without them.

I know Mark was sick, is sick, but it always hurt just the same when he did it, and not just me. The whole family would get sorta sick as he went into one of his fits...especially Mom. She was getting really jumpy there for a while, all the time going to Mass, and she didn't even speak Latin. Then, she slowly started to drink. And then, it got worse.

Mark's not living with us anymore. They took him to a state hospital in Cambridge, and I'm glad. Don't get me wrong. I love my brother, really. It's just that I seen what it was doing to us, my sister and me. Our whole family was going nuts.

Sometimes at night Mark would get up and be sweeping the floors with Mom's vacuum cleaner. "I'm making things right," he'd call out, and we all learned to just turn our radios up loud and let him wind himself down. That was one of the more peaceful things he'd do.

Then one night, after one of his religion friends jumped off a bridge in Wheeling, he just went really mad breaking things. He smashed his fist into our refrigerator; then he threw our vacuum cleaner right through the front window. And then he climbed on through to the porch and started running. We found him in the woods down behind the school—passed out and bleeding, and almost froze. When they woke him up, he started in yelling, "Save yourself! Save yourself!" till they wrapped him up tight and drove off with him. He was seventeen.

I'll tell you the truth. When I seen the way Mom and Dad cried that night and how they really fought the next day, I almost wished Mark had died.

You know, it's not like any of us kids ever had a chance. We just always helped. And we had to understand. Now I feel bad for saying this, but it's true. It's what I'm feeling. I want a life too.

All the kids at school know about Mark, but I don't care about them. He's my brother. I mean, my God, he's my flesh and blood. I love him, really, hopelessly. It's just so hard, that's all.

For a while there, he was doing so good. This doctor in Columbus had us giving him all raw, natural foods...and nothing else. And I mean nothing. The meat and cheese had to be from cows that didn't eat no chemicals. We'd get it up around Sugar Creek in Amish country. And Mark loved it. He said, "For the first time I'm feeling good," and he'd stick to it...eating all that awful stuff and be so sweet, like when he'd buy you something just for no reason whatever. He'd come home from some porch sale and he'd smile at you and you'd find something special on your bed...like you couldn't believe any person could think so much about you. Once he bought me these kelly-green ribbons for my red hair.

Before he went away he'd get real sad sometimes, like he missed burning the candle at both ends. He never did drink or smoke or anything, I mean. He didn't need to. He'd just have these wild maniac times when everything he did was sorta... dancing...exploding like an alarm clock or something. One time he told me he felt like a toilet was always running inside him, only all the time.

Then his Bible friends kept coming around praying with him and singing, real late at night. I used to listen to them and wish they really could save my brother Mark. I'd wonder what it would be like for all of us. Maybe they will heal him yet, but the doctors aren't holding out much light for Mom and Dad. He gets more and more like he isn't there. Maybe you have to get worse before getting better. I don't know, but I do know he doesn't look like my brother anymore. He's so skinny and pale, and he won't even look at me no more.

Anyway, when he would get into what we called his gentle blue periods, he'd sometimes sit rocking on the floor and crying about his lost brother. Nobody ever figured out who he meant, but he'd just say over and over, maybe a hundred times, how he wanted his brother to see. He wanted us all to see, he'd say. That what he said the day we had him taken away.

I have to tell you that I'm seeing this guy, Bob, from Saint Edward's now, and he don't know nothing about Mark, except that I got a brother who's in the hospital somewhere. I went over to meet his folks the other night before the game, and they sure are nice. They don't have no more money that we do or anything really you can put your finger right on, but it's, well, *nice* over there.

I was standing in the kitchen with Bob's mom washing dishes in the sink, and you know she stops washing her roaster just to listen to me while I'm wiping a dish. She just stands there looking nice and staring right into my eyes. I told her lots of stuff I ain't ever told no one, not even myself, like I'm telling you now. And she just took the dish from my hand, which I already dried about five times, and she hugged me tight. I could feel her hand on my hair. I started to cry; then I stopped, 'cause Bob came to take me to the game.

I could hear Mrs. Silverman saying, "Bob, you got a real nice girl here," as he stood at the back door, so then I had to turn away to the car.

One thing you have to understand is that I love my family and especially my brother Mark. I seen other families that seem like they got nothing holding them together. A girl gets an abortion and the parents lock her out of the house. You see a lot of that. Well, we ain't like that. We still care no matter what. Even when Dad walks out at night, I can see Mom hurting. Mark makes us care. It's just this whole big aching I hate, like I know something's there only I can't seem to touch it.

Am I ever going to feel alright? Because I'd like to have my own kids some day, and I want them to grow up liking themselves, and maybe even not afraid to love me.

TWO

The first man I ever went with was a girlfriend's brother. I was clerking then at the Kresgee's, not dating nobody, so when she asked me if I'd go out with her brother just home from the Navy, I said, "Why not."

I'd never seen the guy, but he was five years older and looked pretty slick in his Navy whites. Hell, I can't really count all the Navy guys I've had since then.

Anyway, we met at the Village Bar, had a few drinks, danced a few, and somehow ended up at my place. I remember I was giving him a pretty good French kiss outside the door, and I was going to stop it right there, when he says, "Listen, kid, let's not fool around, huh. I'm leaving tomorrow, so I ain't got the time," and he slips a bill in my hand and holds it there while he keeps rubbing my breast with the other hand. I don't know if I was drunk, or tired, or horny myself, but kinda breathless I just stuffed the bill inside my shorts and pushed open the door.

The next day after coffee, he drove off and I remembered the bill, which I figured was a five for drinks or maybe a ten for the room, but it wasn't. It was a twenty for me. That's when it first hit me, while I was taking a shower and looking across in the mirror. I could make it and take it. I didn't feel nothing for that guy right then, and I didn't feel no guilt either. He had his and I had mine. I quit my job at Kresgee's that weekend and started hanging around the bars—the Village and Captain Doc's.

It was tough at first, but easy too. I was doing it in the backseat of cars and standing up in bathroom stalls. Then I wised up and got an apartment in town close to the bars, and the word got out. I started getting high school boys knocking on my door in the afternoon. They'd show up in a car, send a couple fellows up, and I'd end up taking them on one at a time in my bedroom listening to rock-n-roll. I could have charged them anything, but I didn't...maybe $20, maybe $10. I was doing their girlfriends a favor in a way, you know, breaking them in and all.

And I got really good so as I would have johns who'd keep coming once a week or more—poor saps, some of them, that nobody loved. One guy was trying to be a writer while working at a gas station nights. Stan had the face of a chicken, but could he ever talk. And he'd get me to talk too, like this, where I'd tell him about my family, and he'd say, "Tracey, now that's a story I ought to write." And I'd tell him, now don't you dare.

But, after a while, he kept asking me to marry him, till I had to break it off. I mean, he was giving me half his paycheck every week, and I couldn't afford not to be making it, and we couldn't have ever made it straight. So I told him, one night at the top of the steps, to get lost, that I was making it with a friend. And he started down the steps, then come back up and knocked again. "I'll be back," he says, but I didn't answer. 'Cause I've learned you just can't let anyone get that close to you.

Stan Scott was his name, and I got to admit, I still look in the bookstore to see if he ever made it. Probably not. He'd write these stories where no one is ever happy and nothing even means nothing, and who'd want to read that when it's already what you live?

I had a good friend once. Roxanne. She was in the business and she had this really great laugh, like she enjoyed everything so damn much it made you sit back and laugh too. She had lots of johns, but she got into the candy, if you know what I mean. I though she had everything, and we went and OD'd and wasted it all. One of her johns come and got me in Doc's one night, said, "You better come, take care of Roxy. She sick."

I find her lying in the bathtub like a dead baby bird, her neck twisted funny like it was broke, a look of shock on her face, like she'd see a accident or something. I wrapped her up in a blanket and put her on the bed. I remember sitting there with her waiting for the ambulance, only she was already dead. I didn't know what to do, so pretty soon I'm saying the rosary, over and over, a hundred times.

When they took her away, I just says to myself, "I'm glad it ain't me. I'm glad I ain't dead, though I ain't sure just why."

They buried her up on the hill looking down on this damn valley where nothing changes but the prices. We always got the sound and smells of the mill, and on a windy day the smoke will reach all the way up to Roxy.

I can tell you one thing. It ain't no good being in this business when you get older. The old guys want the young ones. So do the young guys. It's like they're all fucking their youth. Let them. I got my plants, and my cats, and I can always go work at the new K-Mart...even after fifteen years.

One thing I can remember my Dad teaching me is, "There's always another way to skin the cat." I always wondered about the poor cat, though.

THREE

Yeah, I been working here at this Dairy Mart Store for fifteen years, back when it was a Lawsons, and before that a McAllister's milk and lunchmeat place. Now we sell just about everything—from milk in plastic bottles, to fresh sticky buns, to submarine sandwiches we make in the back and you can heat up in our microwave. And we're open 24 hours now. I take the night shift to give the other girls a life.

Hell, you know, here I am a red haired old woman at sixty still slicing baked ham and cheese for anyone that wants it. That's what I spend about 80% of my time doing is slicing. I clocked it once. You ever watch it? That thin blade going round and through, those thin slices coming out then fainting over in your hand. There's a way about it I can't describe. Sometimes it's as sad as the people who come in her at night. And sometimes it's as right as eating bread. But I still count my fingers each time I pull back from that blade. It can be a nasty thing, if you don't play it right—like a lot of men I've knows in my time. Sometimes they'd try to cut you too, only I always had my own razor done up in my hair. I used it too—a couple of times. I had to if I ever wanted to see daylight. Yeah, but that's another life.

I'm a survivor of life itself. There was times when I didn't have no dough to pay the rent or buy bread, and I though to doing it—you know, cashing in my chips. I had a brother once that done just that...hung himself with a pillow case in a mental ward not far from here when I was sixteen.

I wasn't about to. It ain't never come to that. I don't know why, 'cause I ain't got a thing save myself...no family no more, no money in the bank, no lover whose heart I'd break. I suppose they'd miss me here at the store, for about a week, till they got a good replacement. Of course, I got my cats and my plants. Just something makes me hold onto this life—even though it's leftover, I ain't about to throw it away.

You see, I give myself to so many men when I was young—in the business, you know what I'm telling you? I was still good looking in my twenties and early thirties, and I suppose I give a lot of guys a joy ride they won't forget— had 'em reaching for the moon. I know I was always lonely and reaching out for something too. You know, I can see now that all the time I was playing, I was still wishing it was true. And all the time I was just being nudged toward some knowing I was never to know for real.

I even hurt myself for love. If some guy would start to show me some, why I'd take and break him to see if it could last. And it never did. It never could.

The other day I seen a picture of me from when I was a teenager, before my brother killed himself and my mother was taken away. A couple years before I got into the business and become a player. The god awful truth is I didn't even know that kid was me, except for something about her eyes...some sad reaching about those eyes, like she was ashamed to look straight at the camera and afraid not to. And there was this wistiness about her red hair all tied up in those green ribbons, like she was telling herself not to care but couldn't come to believe it.

Well, I'm still here nights, if the wind don't blow me away. I keep going on in spite of all I done to myself, spite of all that's been done to me. Sometimes I stand out front on the corner, about 7 am, after working all night, and I don't care what you say. It's good to smell the morning in the air.

OUTSIDE THE MILLGATE

Walking home from school, I stop at the corner by the gym. Band practice is long over, and again I am the last student to go home. And so I look down the long hill into the deep throat of the steel mill which is always bellowing its shower of noise onto the life of this town. Mingo Junction—for the Indians and the railroads, and we all know Ohio means "beautiful river." Beyond the millgate I look back in and watch the long swing of the crane feeding fresh red ore into the rust-colored blast furnaces which resemble most the leftover bombs from World War II. A lorry car glides north, while two blue engines haul steaming hot ladles of slag south to the piles. Always the motion, always the hard sound of making.

My grandfather rigged those cranes and dumper cars; my uncles works the blast furnace floor; my father is brakeman on those trains. And me—I walk across this street.

Climbing the steps to the back porch, I look down through the trees to the stadium stretched out before the smokestacks in the millyard. My father's windchimes, made from aluminum pipe, are playing, and even the air says there is a game here tonight.

As I open the back door I am swept back by the sickening odor of "permanents" and Mom's corny music. Mom is seated on the kitchen stool in the middle of the room while my aunt buzzes around her with rubber gloves, and her own hair is wrapped in a scarf, like some "haji baba." Mom keeps her head down but manages to say, "Hi, Honey, there's some sugar donuts on the counter by the sink."

I grimace, "Ah—no thanks, ladies. I'd rather breathe than eat," and I make tracks through the mess, my fingers perched like a bird pecking off my nose and Aunt Mae chasing me, "Okay, wise guy," she laughs. "You're next!" And I race out, shouting, "If it's a 'permanent,' how come you have to keep doing it every month?" I leave the sounds of women laughing as I run up the stairs.

Walking down the dark hallway, I think how silence must rise with the heat in a house. My kid sister Jan is in the kitchen playing with her lipstick, her hair in ribbons and curlers, leaning into the mirror.

"Cute!" is all I yell.

"Go away!" she screams, then slams and locks the bathroom door about a second after I close my own. I remember I once locked myself in that bathroom while I snorkeled in the bathtub. I was going for an underwater record when Mom came knocking at the door. When I didn't answer, she went nuts and got Uncle Ray to come over and take the door off the hinges. He pulled me up by the hair, and we all just stared at each other for about a minute, till Mom started to laugh.

In the easy comfort of my room I do not turn on the lights. On the bed are two big envelopes from two colleges which I know we can't afford, wanting me to apply. All I did was fill out this card when I took my SAT's, and I've become a high school fish to which they all throw out their bait. Truth is, I'd be glad to go to any of them if we could afford it. But we can't—though Dad insists we can. There is a whole packet from the U.S. Air Force with a blue jet screaming across the envelope. I glide it gently into the wastebasket. I'd rather work in the mill.

Still with only the dusk for light, I sit on the bed and flip open my cornet case, click—click. It always has that cool metal heft to it as I lift it, bring the mouthpiece home to my lips, and press myself through. My fingers tap lightly, checking the precision of the valves, as my eyes close I stream a favorite phrase from "Sweet Lorain," like sugar icing squeezed onto a cake.

On my chair is the new sheet music I bought at Lombardy Brothers: "Deep Purple." Uncle Satch keeps telling me, "Now, that's a pretty tune—one from my era, you know!" And it really is a nice piece, so I decide to play it in the dark. I slide onto the chair before the open window, prop the music on the wooden stand which Dad made out of a old rocker, and I play...right out the window into the cool mill air.

The music phrases itself so sweetly that after one time through I can almost close my eyes and let go on it. I know I'm somehow singing to life as I play the ending twice with real vibrato. When I open my eyes, there's the millfield spread out like a ledge of scrap iron before the big river and the green West Virginia hills. I know the mill isn't all scrap iron and smoke, I know my family has earned a "good living" there for generations. Believe me, I know all this, and still my eyes and ears don't lie, and my heart does reach for more.

On some rusty fall days I walk out the tracks beside the creek and I stand there casting one stone at a time into the water below. First the splash, then the ripples, then the sinking into the brown water until it can't be seen. And I stand there thinking, *I'll be next*.

This time I play "my song' with eyes open wide upon the town I know, with its rows of old wooden houses, its barking dogs in alleys, its brick chimneys in the Ohio hills. It is just notes and phrases without words, but I play it pure and clear the way a horn can. The cornet is sweeter than the trumpet, but not everyone can hear it. You have to be able to listen and to care. The mouthpiece kisses back.

"Dinner, Sonny," Mom calls, and it's probably the second or third time, because I am just waking up. Dave's radio clock says 5:05, and I have to be at the band room by 5:45, so I go down with sleep still hanging from my eyes.

Somehow Mom has chased the cold odor of the Toni Home Permanent with the warm aroma of cabbage rolls. They're what's left of the batch she made on Monday, but with fresh mashed potatoes, warm bread, and coffee—they're *Choice*. Dad is on the second shift, and it's just Mom, Janis, and me, so we all sit at one end of the table. It's funny sitting in Dad's seat, the Captain's chair. I can feel him in the wood of the seat, see where his hands have worn smooth the arms. My older brother Dave is off studying to become a minister in some Presbyterian college in Tennessee. He got a scholarship to Maryville and works cleaning the cafeteria at night—Old Mr. Responsible—and I miss him.

"That was a nice song you play, Sonny. I like it when you play a song," Mom says this while she is buttering her bread. She always breaks he bread before she butters it and says we should too.

"Which one, Mom?" I ask to prolong the praise, "That new 'Deep Purple' song?"

"Yes, that one too. But what's the name of that last one you played?"

Now taking a real compliment has never been easy for me. I get this scary, full feeling, like I'm walking across a railroad bridge at night.

"That's just some song he made up," Janis laughs. "Gee whiz, he plays that thing night and day!"

"I call it 'Daybreak.'" Then leaning towards Janis, "And some little people in this house have awfully big ears and mouths," and I twitch her buns till she slaps my hand away.

"Sonny, your father says he'll try to work it so his crew is hauling back ladles around the time of the halftime show," and Mom passes more potatoes while I nod, "He says the trouble is the other men want to see the game," and she looks away at her plate.

"I guess I know that," I say, like it means something, and we eat together in kitchen light.

Our band marches down the hill from school as though we are going to disappear into the mill or the river, but actually we march along Commercial Street under the railroad overpass and along the Bottoms into the stadium parking lot. At the gate, Mr. Morton calls for a roll-off—a long, then short whistle, four sharp drum taps, and we launch into our fight song. I am playing automatically, but still I get a chill.

I march in the first row, right guard, and right behind Marcia Lane, the majorette who moved here from Pittsburgh last year. My God, her dark red hair ignites me even more than her white, gleaming legs. She could lead me and my row right into the river and I'd follow. I am thinking all this when the band stops quickly and I keep marching right into Marcia. Stumbling, I grab her around the waist to keep her from falling, yet she turns her smallness against me and I feel myself falling, like a waterfall inside my heart.

"Sonny!" she laughs inside of herself, then faces me as I stumble still for my footing.

"Let's get hold of ourselves, shall we?" Morton says to us, and we turn to see the hole band in a silent laughing fit.

"I'm sorry," I blurt out, a half lie.

When we line up across the field at halftime, the other band is already doing its show. The stands are a blur of stadium light in the shadows of the mill. Then, as if on cue, the fluorescent glow of the Bessemer furnace lines the buildings like a silhouette painting in the night. Marcia is standing beside me and I say, "Millflower."

"What did you say?" she smiles toward my face.

"I said, it's like a millflower, that orange-pink light around the dark buildings and us here inside." And she smiles again like she can feel it growing too.

"My father left my mother," she tells me softly. "That's why I'm living with my mom at my grandmother's." I am touching her sleeve. "I don't know," she sighs, "I hardly know anyone here, and sometimes I just want to cry all day, you know."

I hardly get out a "Yes, I do." I love hearing her speak so much. Then, the other band begins "The Stars and Stripes Forever," and the order goes out to "Line up!" I find myself touching the music of her hair. "Marcia," I hear myself speak, "Can I walk you home after the game?"

In a breath, "Sure, Sonny," and she runs off, "I'll meet you by the steps." Her hair and skirt bounce together in the light around my heart.

I blow air through my cornet to warm it up and press valves randomly to loosen them. Standing there on the far forty yard line I turn from the stands to the fence and the millyard in the dark. For the first time I hear the mill siren whining. One learns not to hear things in a milltown. There is no train though, only the distant clank of gondolas jolting against each other. I look back into the stadium lights and suddenly feel empty and full all at once.

Four taps and we are into "When the Saints..." already halfway across the field..."Go Marching In."

At the band room, Morton motions me over. I am trying not too obviously to hurry so I don't miss Marcia, who has slipped into the girls' lockerroom. I snap my case closed, circle behind the clarinets, and head towards the door.

Morton has this serious face on, like he's just had a drink of Clorox of something, so I follow him into one of the practice rooms.

"Sonny, I'm afraid I've got some bad news," and his hand is on my shoulder, guiding me down to a chair. He sits beside me like in a practice lesson, "I just talked to your uncle on the phone." I can feel my world melting into the darkness outside. "There's been a accident in the mill, and, well, your father's been hurt." My whole body goes limp, so I hardly hear him say, "Your uncle will be by to pick you up in a few minutes."

Something inside me forces a breath out--a senseless puff to keep my insides from imploding, "O-kay," I say, and wait out the silence.

"Just sit a while," says Mr. Morton, pressing my shoulder; then he goes outside to get the others out of the building. We've got ten minutes to get out.

I get up and walk numbly to the window. In the cold glass I see my father's face, his deep brown eyes and rugged cheeks, his mouth about to speak...and then it is Marcia's face. I turn to see her standing at the door, gazing at me.

I open the door. "Let's wait outside," I say, then hear myself, "My dad's been hurt in the mill."

"I know," she whispers and wraps her arm around mine as we walk outside.

Soon it is she who is crying as she leans against my shoulder, her soft hair a pillow for my cheek. I can feel her body shake against mine, and I want to live and die at once.

I just hold her.

At my father's funeral we all stand around the flowered rooms and try to talk. All these people--family and neighbors, people from church, my school friends--I know they are good to come, but I've told the story of the broken ladle and the hot iron spill so many times I can't do it again. None of it makes sense, anyway. It wasn't supposed to happen and it did. Nothing else to say.

Mom is holding up really well, although she seems tired inside, and we're all just numb with details. Dave is home and helping us bear up. He wants to say the words at the service tomorrow, and I want him to. Aunt Mae is taking charge of the food the neighbors send. Janis stays up at the house, mostly, but she's been to see Dad twice with the family. "That ain't Daddy," she whispered to me yesterday, and I didn't know what to say. Right now I feel like Dad's drifting around somewhere near, and I begin to seen him more in all of us.

Uncle Satch comes out to stand with me on the front porch. He looks towards the mill and says, "Railroaders are a superstitious bunch, you know. You won't see many of them here, or at the funeral for that matter. They're spooked." I look into Uncle Satch's face and wish he would cry a little for me, for us all. This grief seems like such a long road right now.

Last night Marcia and her mom showed up. They were both really nice. She had her hair down long and wore a black suit with lace around her neck. I fell right into her eyes, and we held each other for five minutes out back. Her touch was like music in the dark, and we both cried while the mill roared.

On the front porch of the funeral home I discover that I can look across the street, over the tracks, to the stadium and the steel mill. Inside the house is what's left of a good man and the gentle sound of people trying to comfort each other. When I look around the side of the funeral home I can see our house two yards back, and I can hear Dad's wind chimes and see the window of my room. I want to go there and play my cornet into the night.

Dad was born in Grandma's house two doors over, lived for two years in West Virginia, then back to our house. He and Mom lived their lives in this town, never more than a block from each other. Now the mills are laying off, only working part of the year. The old timers are being retired early and sit around on benches, mumbling, "It ain't the same." And it isn't, but who is to blame?

I'm glad Dad won't have to watch the mills die. He'd have fought to save them; this valley was his life. I don't know, really; it just seems that for anything to get born in this life, another thing has got to die.

As for me—I'm right here, right now, walking across this street.

INSIDE THE SMOKE

"Are you going to quit or what?"

And she dropped the eggs onto his plate, set the skillet onto the stove, then leaned against the sink, drinking her second cup of coffee. Her dark hair was still wild about her small face.

Michael's eyes traced from her slipper up the line of her body, soft inside a blue furry robe and as familiar as his food.

"I'm not saying that I'm quitting. I'm just telling you what he said to me." And he focused from her face to her dark intent eyes, "'You better work this double, Pitts, while you can still got the work.' That was it, and he walks out the locker room door leaving me halfway in the shower, like he was some kind of football coach."

"Michael," she pleaded, "this will be the third time you've been laid off this year." She set her cup firmly inside the sink and turned to face him, "Now what kind of a life is this, really?" with all the weight on the 'really.'

The gray room silence covered his plate, so that he felt the deep burning in his stomach again, yet he sat there still as a deer inside a brake of trees. Then the phone rang, and Laurel's voice didn't even bother to change as she spoke to her mother, "Yeah. Well? Mom, I got a wast to get done, and Michael just worked a double, so the baby's all mine today...I'll see if I can come down this afternoon. Okay?"

Michael began to butter his toast, slowly as the butter began to tear the bread, so that he folded the bread and pressed the hard butter between his fingers. Sometimes even food doesn't work. A bright morning sunlight bleached the room, and he watched his hand tremble on the juice glass so that he had to set it down. He couldn't tell if it was from the work or the threat of no work.

Laurel was still talking on the phone, "Listen, I'll be there when I get there, Mom. God, I can't do everything," and she hung up.

"Michael, what are we going to do?"

The trees outside his bedroom window cast a forest of shadows on the walls, yet he slept the restless sleep of overwork. For a long time all he could see was the blast furnace troughs, glowing like a dirty sunset. For a long time his back still carried the wheelbarrow across the furnace floor. "Work makes work on the blast furnace," his foreman would say. Once the furnace is tapped, for thirty minutes the steel pours itself into waiting torpedoes, as the molten slag pours itself into open-mouthed ladles. Then it begins again—clean up, reline the troughs with sand, begin again—the only rest comes while the furnace is running. The men run the furnace and the furnace runs the men.

Finally Michael dreamed a dream of rest, of soft sleep inside the rain. He and his father sat inside a field tent and watched it rain on the river like forever.   When he woke, he knew the house was empty. Laurel had taken Beth to her mom's, who knew for what. He lay there smelling his own sweat pressed inside the pillow. Still time for more, so he climbed back inside, but this time there was no dream, and he slept a dead man's sleep.

Laurel's mom was lost in her 60's, without a husband to care or care for. She had lived on alone in the old house which daily settled into certain decay. "My God," Laurel would say, "The place is over a hundred. Why don't they make it a monument?" and her mom just laughed quietly. Even their garden had turned from crisp vegetables to fierce weeds. Only the dusty maples renewed themselves each spring.

Laurel climbed the basement stairs with a load of clothes. She stepped before the television, "Mom, you have to remember to push the button on this dryer, that's all. Set it, close it, then push the button *on*." And she stared at her mother to be sure she was listening.

"But the other one always started when you shut the door." Every week she made this same protest. "And, besides, I thought I smelled smoke."

"Just press the button, Mom. Alright? Can you do that?" and she lugged the clothes upstairs to the bedroom.

The afternoon rain sent a soft breeze through he rooms so that the old woman rose from her lounge chair to check the baby in her crib. They needed a crib in both houses now for when they both worked.

The baby slept softly before the window so that the old woman bent forward and pressed her face close on the baby's blanketed bottom.

"Jesus, you scared me!" gasped Laurel, back in the room now. "Mother, PLEASE don't wake Beth," and she was already out the door still talking, while the old woman looked from the mother to the child, then retreated to her television.

Outside, the smoke drifted over the trees down river, as Laurel drove off. A mill siren signalled another shift, and the old woman thought, "It's time for the news."

For days Michael had hunted the paper for any news of the new Saturn auto plant. General Motors had been "deliberating" for months now where to build their new auto plant.

How would they decide? Michael tried to reason it. He had already decided to move wherever it was built. "Anywhere within three states," he had said to Laurel, "Anywhere within our reach." And there it was, "General Motors Delays Decision on Saturn Plant Till December," three more months of not knowing and the smoke of more rumors and news stories. The taunting mail from school children, the caravans from hometowns, all of it had proven useless.

Michael closed the paper, "I'd rather start my own farm." He spoke to the air, "I'd rather be in a field under a sky somewhere till my bones and the stones are one."

Wherever he looked he saw what needed to be done—dishes stacked in the sink, patched plaster to be painted, fresh wood outside to be cut and stacked for the winter. Thank God for therain, he thought and drifted into the little living room. He plugged in a tape of a movie they'd seen on AMC and stretched himself before the couch. He liked lying on the floor where the ground was close and familiar. The room grew comfortable, then faded with television light. Dom DeLuise was coaching another smaller man on how to manage his place as he ate from it. Michael remembered a river campfire when his father lay fried catfish onto his plate beside the bread and said, "Let it soak up the grease. You can pull the bones out all in one piece." He smiled while the actor ate.

Outside, a car door shut—their Ford van. Laurel would walk in any moment. Michael gathered up the room.

"Well, Michael, I see you been working your butt off." She really didn't want to start in but couldn't stop the scene from rolling. She hadn't stopped moving all day.

Michael reached into the closet behind her for his light jacket. "I gotta go. I gotta go talk to some guys about what's happening in the mill." He didn't look at her, but patted her tight-jean rump and rolled out the door, touch and go. "But I just got here," fell from her lips, but he was already down the steps. "See ya," he called from the car door. "Michael," hung on her lips like a taste of saccharin. She lit a cigarette and sat in the glow of kitchen chrome while the baby talked.

Michael drove slowly—not really certain where to go. He passed the new low income houses nested in with the old. He passed the budget bread store, the corner Dairy Mart. A group of teenagers in jeans and leathers stood in the doorway of the Laundromat watching it rain. He passed the green Dodge junked on Sinclair Street. It was all a movie he had seen a hundred times, perhaps he had made it. But he watched it still, took it in and waited for the point to arrive.

At Patsy's Dinner beyond the slag plant he found a parking place in back. It was Tuesday—Spaghetti Night—and he whiffed the oregano sauce and garlic bread, and he pushed his way inside the doors.

The booths were all packed with families—their night to eat out. For some reason Patsy's crowd always ate with their jackets on and talked loud as if at home. It was almost too bright and open for an restaurant, but it was Patsy's, the hometown dinner. Michael nodded to a couple, waved at a buddy eating with his kids, "Hey, Mike, we're wolfing the macaronis."

"Yeah, I see," he tried to laugh and recognized the new waitress as a girl he went to school with. Ten years ago she had been a majorette; now she was hauling platters at Patsy's.

He stopped before an empty counter seat. The old guy on his left nodded. He was eating the dinner special—the hot roast beef sandwich with french fries and gravy. On the other side was a fellow Michael knew from the mill, sipping coffee as he read the evening paper. Franketti had just gotten divorced, and this was where he took his meals. Franketti rubbed his cigarette into the little aluminum ashtray already full of butts.

"Sit her down, Pitts," he nodded to the empty stool. "We won't bite you. Will we, Pops?"

The short haired waitress set down a place of spaghetti and meatballs across the counter, tore off a check, slipped it under the plate, turned and asked, "Coffee, Michael?"

"Sure, Betsy," picking up the menu. For the first time he wondered what he was doing there. Laurel would have supper in an hour or so. He hadn't come to eat.

All the counter seats held men—off their shift. Michael knew the routine: work all morning—layoff for lunch—pace out the afternoon (maybe do two runs on the furnace)—shower up—then roll out to the mill bar for drinks and talk, maybe play a few numbers till five—then drive down to Patsy's for supper, then home to watch the tube and fall asleep.

For a moment he felt he should leave, go home to Laurel and the baby, maybe drive up to the mall and walk around. Gazing at the menu, he played out this little movie inside his head. They would come home, put the baby in her crib, then climb between fresh sheets to lie like the lovers they had been.

"What'll it be?" Michael didn't answer. "Hey, dreamboy, you goin' to order or not?"

"I'll just have some apple pie with ice cream," and he set the menu back in its place behind the sugar.

"Okay, Hon," Betsy said and lay a fork beside his cup. "Cheer up," as she reached across the counter, "It's my birthday." She brushed his cheek with her plump fingers.

No one caught it, her way of shooting down the blues which her guys trailed in with them, like dark muddy tracks. She'd told him that one night drinking coffee on her break. "You know, Hon, most of our worries is just air," and she turned her head to blow a plume of smoke—"Just like that."

Michael had felt a laugh deep inside, the kind a kid has when a giant climbs out of a tiny car, the kind of laugh a person has after landing safe on the ice, like Beth when he throws her up and catches her.

"Hey, Betsy," called Franketti, "How about a birthday kiss?"

Setting the pie down without turning, she shot back, "It's *my* birthday, not *yours*." And when Franketti let out a moan, she simply slapped her rump, kept her hand there, and fired back—"Kiss this!" The whole counter burst into a laugh, even Franketti who began to bark.

Michael felt the laugh go down his throat to his stomach. He loved it here where he could smile and drink coffee without its burning his gut. He scooped up a rich spoonful of vanilla and dropped it into his cup to cool and sweeten it.

"Hey, Mike," it was Franketti again. "You hear anything about a layoff?" He talked without looking up from his food.

"You bet your sweet ass there's one comin.'" It was the red faced guy across the counter, a clerk down at the BOF office. Franketti set his knife beside his bread. "I get so I can feel it comin.' Just about the time we get goin' good, about to catch our second wind, they pull us up and it's back to go."

"Only we won't be collectin' no $200 this time around, 'cause the union says the compensation funds is all eaten up." There was this strange need to think and say the worst, as if it prepared them for something.   Michael was glad not to get into the talk. Sometimes it was the man talking, and sometimes it was the mill. Tonight he felt his heart batted across the counter by others.

Finally, Franketti leaned way forward collecting attention around the counter, and said low, "I'll tell you something you men already know. This industry is SCREWED." Then looking around at each man, "We're a dying breed, a bunch of damn dinosaurs, that's what we are, by God."

"You said it, man. Steelmaking's been screwed by everybody till we're a dead whore. And nobody gives a shit."

The old guy beside Michael suddenly turned to stare at the two men, then surprised everyone by speaking, "That mill there," motioning broadly with his arm, "That mill was damn good to me and mine for over fifty years." He stared around at the blank faces, "Maybe you men don't know how to love her anymore," and he rose to go.

"Yeah, old man," it was red face, "and these days that mill can't get it up no more than you can."

"Hey, easy..." Betsy hushed them, and Michael saw that the old man had left his pipe beside his half-eaten supper. He grabbed it and caught up with him at the register.

"Mister, you forgot this." The two men faced each other a long moment. Then the old man reached out pressing Michael's extended hand.

"Don't you forget," he said, "We ain't already dead, and we didn't live for nothing." Still holding onto Michael's hand—the pipe strangely cupped between their palms. "Them others is just blind with bitterness. Don't you believe in their nightmares, boy. There's still a dream there."

Betsy had caught up from behind, "You okay, Dad? Don't take no crap from those guys. If they had something, they wouldn't know it till it was gone." And she pressed a kiss into his hair.

Standing there in the light, Michael began to feel again that he was a character in a movie, in several movies at once. For a second he froze the frame, while he lay three dollars on the counter, then trucked out the door.

Those were good people in there. He knew them when times were better, when they would slap each other on the back and buy a round. Now, all were hanging onto whatever they already had, like in the sinking Titanic. He'd watched that movie when he was a kid, and his mother once pointed out a man from Uniontown who had been on that boat as a kid and swum to a lifeboat by hanging onto his mother's neck. But that too was another's person's story. What Michael wanted was to start his own.

As the wipers flapped across his van windows he looked at the dripping trees. Parked on Cemetery Hill, he could see his father's grave lush and green before the heavy headstone. Michael had them carve that hammer and saw into the headstone for all those years he had run to get his father tools, held a flashlight under a car or a ladder against the house as he fixed things. What Michael wanted now was to talk to his old man, to ask him what to do with his life.

Inside he felt alone and empty. He wound down the window to feel the rain on his face and shirt. They couldn't spoil the rain. His face was dripping when he opened the door and stood outside before the tombstone; his clothes felt cold and close.

"Dad," he hesitated, now knowing whether to think or just speak as the sky flashed up near the television tower. "I've tried it your way. It doesn't work anymore, Dad. This valley is closing in." He needed to believe that. "I can't make it, and I can't let go." His breathing came in gasps, "I don't forget you, Dad, but I can't be you." Michael listened with wonder at his words.

"That valley there...those mills..." but he couldn't make himself say that it was over, that the life of the valley gone for good. Something held him back from the murder of those words. "I don't know. I don't know. I don't know which way to go." In the darkness he grabbed for breath. Surely this was a movie or strange dream of his, yet he pressed it closer.

Lighting flashed across the valley again and again. The thunder a distant rumble as he climbed back inside the van and rolled the window up. Seated there, breathing hard, caught in the exhaustion of his nerves he began to see.

Above the hill of his father's grave was an old hickory blowing in the storm. He watched it take the wind and rain and began to remember another hickory up river where he and his father had camped and fished. In the morning his father had taken the boy's hand and pressed it on the bark. Then he lay a leaf across his palm, "This is hickory," he said and lead him out from the branches to a sapling. "What kind of tree is this?" he asked.

Michael remembered pressing the leaf from his palm against the young tree's leaf, till he himself said, "Hickory."

"When the old tree is dying it sends out shoots," his father's words, "So the new trees go out as they must, yet they grow from the roots of the old." And his father stared into his young eyes.

Michael's eyes now closed on an image of trees, an old truth buried beneath the skin. He felt his own blood pulsing like the sound of rain inside his head. He tasted the rain on his lips and saw traces of his own breath on the windows. He smelled his own wetness inside the van.

Slipping the van into gear he headed back down the hill, laughing as he drove, all the way home.

A YEAR IN BOULDER

I remember those first days as part of a sunny dream—
Boulder in September. I caught a ride from Toledo with a
college friend. He picked me up outside of Tony Packo's on
a rainy night. I was saying so long to my friends and heading
West to work for Greenpeace at the foot of the Rocky
Mountains. Troy was headed for a computer job in the silicon
valley of Livermore making little nuclear detonators, I'm
sure. We joked about the absurdity of it all at the McDonalds,
Wendy's, and gas giving truckstops across Indiana, Illinois,
Iowa, and Kansas. Twenty-six hours of driving his Thunder-
bird, smoking his Marlboros, and talking his life. When he let
me off in downtown Boulder, we just grinned at each other,
and I said, "Hey, Troy. Have a good life."

I remember, Boulder seemed a pretty crazy place
then, lots of long hairs, the jangle of foreign voices, lots of
little shops for books and beads, futons and coffee, compact
discs and ski's. Somehow I made it to the little Greenpeace
office exactly at noon on the day I said I would arrive. The
office was a storefront on a sidestreet, and Mark and Jill were
the first Greenpeacers that I met. Two weathered activists in
charge of the Denver-Boulder region. They were so cool
about the whole scene, really. "You can start tonight," Jill
said, then smiled. "You'll earn enough to stay alive." Through
wire-rimmed glasses she checked me over as if detecting
rust, then winked, "And, hey, let's hope you make a little
difference. You know, make a few waves in the foothills.
We're going to stop this nuclear dumping that's become
rampant at Rocky Flats." I stood there simply smiling into
her sincere green eyes. I hadn't talked to anyone this intense
or sincere since I entered college.

Mark, a rugged "thirty something" in jeans and a vest, spoke right at you. He handed me a clipboard with a bunch of pamphlets. "*These*, my friend, are your tools," he said, "these and your ability to think and talk straight up. Read them before you go out, so you know what you're about." I held them all in my hand like a spread of cards, and he motioned me to the couch.

"Steve, I'll tell you, it's not easy out there. You'll get your face blown off by the slamming doors of the people you're out to help. Your feet will be singing the blues come nightfall, and you'll learn quick enough how the mountain cold drops like a curtain with the sunsets." He watched the smile fading from my face. "But you'll make a lot of contacts, buddie, and let's hope a few friends for the earth."

I mumbled something dumb like, "Lord knows we can use them." I think he could see how road weary I was, 'cause he told me to sack out till 2:30 when the group would start coming in to get coffeed up for the long haul from 2:30 to 7:30.

"We want to get folks when they're home, and we want to be out of their neighborhoods before sunset."

I lay back on the leather couch; it had more cracks than my aunt Mae's face. I began to wonder what kind of a job this was and what a business degree from a working class school like Toledo University had to do with any of this. Hell, who really cared! Since graduation in May this was the first real work I had taken on, my moving here...the first real choice I had made. "Gotcha," I said, nestling myself into a couch corner, "Just push my button when you're ready."

That night...I'll never forget it. After a long wasted run of housing projects and a suburban hill district, we buzzed back to Mark's place for the night. A gang had come along for their Friday night party. It was pretty mellow though, lots of candles around a fireplace, a little guitar playing—strictly acoustic—and some strong coffee and cheap mountain wine. Pretty soon people started drifting down the hallway—boats headed into their bedroom ports. And I, I was left on another couch, my dock for the night. It was like one of those days that seem like a week, so I just let go and for a while fell into a deep bowl of sleep.

"My mother is a xerox machine," she sang, softly strumming a guitar before the fire. "My father is a train." And she laughed so that her teeth danced between her lips. She was just rocking gently there on a pillow in the glow. I don't think she even knew I was in the room. "And I'm a little magnet...a copy on the tracks of life." She wasn't really playing any chords, just lightly ringing the strings. Then she set it down and drew her fingers up through her frizzed blonde hair. She just shook it at the flame. "Booga—Booga!" she sang to the snapping light as it touched her tan face.

"Booga—Booga, back to you," I spoke softly. Now there were two of us in that dim room.

She turned and I could see her eyes shining, only I wasn't sure if it was from something she felt or if they were just wet from taking in all the smoke from that roach in the bowl at her side.

"Who—are—you?" she floated my way, making a calico cat face. I didn't speak. "I'm sorry," she said. "I thought I was alone," only she had this thin African blouse on so that I could just see her fair breasts aglow in the warm light.

Silence, and then I asked, "What were you singing?"

"Something I just made up and something I don't want to talk about. Are you a friend of Jerry's?" I never did find out who Jerry was.

"You could say that," smiling into the dark, "But then, you could say I was anybody's friend." The only sounds for a while were the crackling of the flame, some distant music, and her soft breathing.

"I can dig that. Really," she smiled, turning back to the flame, then adding, "If *you* can."

We just sat there a while, her rocking, me motionless; then when she stood up I could see she had a black cat on her lap. She turned and walked toward me...getting smaller inside her shadow, but she was real alright. "Joy" someone had called her. She dropped herself at my feet on the couch, and for the first time I could read her small sad face. Her eyes you couldn't tell, from the stuff she was doing, but her face looked young but tight. The skin seemed weathered, smoothed and etched. She folded her legs under her, in the Boulder tuck, and stared back at the light. "I think about my family back in Phoenix sometimes, you know...five hundred miles away from home...I can hear the whistle blow... five hundred miles." I was starting to drift down those miles in the soft wind of her voice when she laughed, "How about you, guy? You got any folks tonight...to speak of?"

I could feel her rubbing my feet then, and I would have started getting sleepy, if my mind hadn't been aflame. She snuck up behind me on the couch and I could feel her warmth against my tired back. She smelled of flowers, I swear, and I tried to remember seeing her earlier in the light. It didn't matter, as she began rubbing her head softly between my shoulders.

"Yeah," I heard myself say. "I've got one of those little tight-assed families back in Toledo, Ohio. And I bet they're home wondering what their boy has gone and done with his life. I'm just glad to have blown off that whole scene on the trip out here, you know!" I really didn't know where all that big bitterness was coming from, just that it was *there* now that I was *here*.

She started petting my arm with her long fingers. "You're new," she sighed, as though that answered something. I was burning inside and felt like getting up. I felt like shaking her awake. I felt like kissing her eyes and hair in the sweet mouth of darkness.

As our lips parted, she pressed her fingers against my forehead and began rubbing soft circles into my temples. A tenderness gently rippled beneath my skin.

"We're all going somewhere," she finally said, then sighed against my hair, "Going out...or coming in..." The room echoed and then, "Why regret any...thing?"

On the back porch the next morning I watched the sun come up over Boulder, soft clouds moving through the trees. Man, you truly knew you were in the mountains. Denver was like a pile of shiny coins stretched out at the foot of the Rockeys, but Boulder was *there*, Boulder was *in*.

Sitting on the wooden steps I felt clean and close. My hand grazed the wood and felt the warmth of the sun on boards. I remember it was so early you could still hear the birds above the rumble of traffic. I just listened for a while, just coasting inside the moment when I heard the door open and Mark came out carrying two brown crock mugs. "Here, Steve," he said. We both stared into the steamy blackness. It was that time before thought. Finally, we both said, "Coffee."

We stood in the mountain air drinking the steaming coffee, and then he said, "Today, we'll find you some digs."

"Yeah," I answered, "some digs."

"Up the hill is a Greenpeace house. We can start there."

We drank more coffee, but I could tell he wasn't real sure of me nor I of him. It was a pretty big leap I had made from the rattle of traffic on Monroe Street in Toledo to the quiet pool I felt on Fuller Street in Boulder. Mark stood up and shook his long hair back. "Nice—nice—day!" I decided not to echo this one.

"How'd it go last night? You find a place to stretch out?"

I knew my grin was a broadcast, but I honestly couldn't stop it. I hadn't been with a woman for months, and suddenly here was this Joy creature taking to me like a silk shirt or something. "You *could* say that," I laughed like your regular college joe. "I made it home there with one of the *ladies*." I was standing in the yard nodding and grinning at the grass, while Mark checked me over again like my zipper was down.

"What's wrong?" I asked.

"Nothing," he said, then shook his head just a little, just enough. "You're just still carrying parts of Toledo around with you, that's all. You'll set them down when you're ready."

I remember thinking how *everyone* was so philosophical out here, so layed back and cool about it all, but I still sensed a put-down coming. We went inside to the smell of toast and the crunch of kitty litter by the door. No lights...no blinds...just a steady stream of mountain sunlight.

I didn't see Joy again—knew she would probably sleep through till noon—so Mark and I headed out to his Jeep. "Bring the rucksack," he yelled from the yard. "We'll find you those digs right now."

I remember I looked around the porch, back in the hall, but all that was there was my green duffle bag and backpack. "The *what*?" I called back dumbly.

"Your rucksack," he laughed pointing at my stuff at my feet. Damn. Did they all talk like a cattle drive out here or what?

As he pulled out, turning to check the traffic on my side, he slapped my thigh, "Never read Kerouac's *The Dharma Bums* huh?"

"No," I confessed, "But last year I read *Winnie-the-Pooh.*" He didn't laugh. So I quickly added, "I did read his *On the Road* in honors lit last year. It was a seminar called 'The Beat Movement and American Romanticism.' Lots of Emerson and Thoreau, Whitman, then a leap into the 1950's to Ferlinghetti and Kerouac."

We were pulling into some traffic at the light. "Who else you do in that course? I'm interested. Ginsberg?"

"Yeah, we read *HOWL* and something else... *The Fall of America*—Good old prophetic visionary stuff—expand and contract/ expand and contract. And then we did Philip Whalen and Gregory Corso—two happy poets, one mad on Zen the other on Shelley and New York."

Mark nodded as he pulled up to the crest of the hill near the university. Then he shifted into fourth. "You a lit major, or what? I forget."

"Actually, business management..." It sounded funny even to me now, "God knows why. I think I'll lose my degree just by being out here." For the first time, Mark let a smile crack through. I remember we were on Canyon Road yet inside the city.

"I couldn't get all my requirements in, so I took another year...lots of good stuff for myself. I think that's when I lost my capitalist edge."

"Good move, partner," he said and slowed before a funny brick building. It looked like a church and an old school. "This here is the Naropa Institute." We were on Arapahoe Avenue.

My face was an empty bowl. Mark stared into it dumbly.

"Home of 'The Jack Kerouac School of Disembodied Poetics'—ever hear of it?" He was making it easy, but my ignorance had grown to monster size.

"His Beat buddies come here in July each year for a month of celebrating old Jack's spontaneous and heart breaking prose. You just missed it." His eyes showed he was really doing this for my benefit, and yet I still wasn't getting it.

"No kidding, the whole bunch out here in Boulder. I didn't know they were still alive."

"Yep. Some are." He started moving again, "the whole hairy literati celebrating Buddhism and the Beat in downtown Boulder. You'll love it!" And then he looked my way and added, "If you're still around."

He stuck in a tape of John McCutcheon singing an old union song, "Step by Step," and wound the jeep around the morning streets in the music.

What he'd called the Greenpeace House turned out to be a rented house where six Greenpeace canvassers lived in commune, sharing expenses and food, weed and music, lots of fresh coffee and ideas. We had two big dogs in that small house. I was number seven and was given a sleeping bag and the living room's Salvation Army couch during the nights— another of the couches of my life, yet it was a place and a space to be and begin.

Those next months were blessed with time and friends. I'd wake up each morning, fetch a cup of coffee, then lie down with a book and read till noon. I'd talk with Pete and

Jake, Julie or Richelle, then go out to hit the Greenpeace trail on the streets of Denver and then Boulder.

I remember the first book I read there was Mark's worn copy of *The Dharma Bums*, Kerouac's fictional account writ after he and poet Gary Snyder had been climbing the Sierras. Here was Kerouac, city boy not at all unlike myself, making the big Nature scene. The book got inside of me, you know, and it sang of a different kind of journeying. I laughed when I came to the section on the rucksack rebellion—Snyder's own dream of a nation of folks brought up on earth values, a love for the dance of life, and a real respect for the tribe. I began living it.

I walked around with that stuff inside me, climbed the hills around Boulder with Mike and Sue, and Laura, a girl from Chicago that I began falling in love with. We ate little sacks of trail mix, swam in cool streams, talked about how the world was and should be. Laura had these deep dark eyes and a quick smile that always showed her teeth; she was so easy to talk with heart to heart, and we started to share our lives and our plans. We learned to meditate together at Naropa and walked home in sweet silence.

Other days I'd take the dog out and hang around the park, lie on a picnic table reading Kerouac novels and Snyder's books of poems. Sometimes I'd just watch the faces of the people in the park. It was such a full rich time, and I could just listen to people talk and be there with them or be watching a bird streak across the sky and know it without thinking or naming it—just be it inside myself. It all comes back as a slow motion film full of soft dissolves suffused with light.

I remember one time I was lying on the back porch floor looking up at the sky through the trees. I was remembering some lines from *Dharma Bums* where he quotes the

Chinese poet Han Shan about the mountain being a house without beams or walls, with all the doors left open and the hall a big blue sky. It made a kind of Zen heart sense that way. And I remembered too lying around my house in Toledo while my parents worked and my sister was in school and my only adventure seemed to be in watching old movies or a new videotape. Laura was inside making oatmeal cookies, and I remember her bringing the whole big blue crock bowl out to me to see if it looked right. She let me taste some sweet dough from a wooden spoon, and I first kissed her there on the steps.

I made enough money those first months to pay my share, plus enough pocket cash to see a few good experimental films at the university. It was all mind blowing stuff and it kept me out of any trouble. I didn't ever see Joy again, though I often thought about her and her strange little song. She drifted back like the opening scene of a movie.

Then one night Mark and I were logging reports and I was telling him about Laura's teaching me to meditate. He asked me how I liked Kerouac now, and I said just fine. And then he said something I'll never forget, "Yeah. The real tragedy is he couldn't find enough to keep him from drinking old death."

"What you saying? Kerouac died of a burst vein in Florida in 1969." It was true. Why bring him down like this?

"Take it easy," he said, "If you know that much, you should also know how he just stopped writing and began drinking himself to death in Lowell, Massachusettes, around '66. That big hearted man just couldn't stop beating himself to death. But that was his trip, man. We all have our own demons. Don't we?"

I swallowed some hard silence, then agreed. "Right," I said, but I was no longer so sure of anything. And right then, for some crazy reason, I asked Mark if he'd seen or heard from Joy. He looked up long enough to read my troubled face and said, "She's gone, Man...went back home to Phoenix. *Had to!*"

I remember how I was about out the door when I turned again, "What you mean 'had to'?"

He just stopped logging reports and said, "Steve, can you wait around till the others go?"

"No problem," I called back on my way to the head, there was no hurry. I figured I'd wash up while I waited. In the sink mirror I recognized an older person there. My face was weathered now and smooth with those dark etched lines. I liked what I saw. The cold splash of water on my cheeks only felt right, and made my head more clear. I knew my face. I had been travelling to the home in myself. The soap smelled fresh like Boulder. As I stared at it I must have been squeezing cause it slipped onto the floor.

When I walked back into the room Mark was zipping the cash bag which he locked in the overnight safe.

"How about a cup of coffee?" he asked.

"Sure," I said, "Let me get it."

When I handed him the cup, he motioned me to a chair. "Look here, partner, I asked you to stay, see. Cause...well, you asked about Joy." His voice strained as the words plodded out. "Not many people know this, see. Joy is gone, so we need to forget her, but we also need to remember her."

I was thinking about how he must have loved her or something, and of how Laura would be waiting dinner for me. "I didn't know what was going on between you," I said, searching for the connection to all this, but Mark was staring back at me all hurt or mad or something.

"What?" I said, "I figured you were saying you two had something special."

"No," he said. "That ain't it. You don't get it, partner. And what you don't know can hurt you...especially here."

"Okay. God, I admit it. I don't get it. Please, spit it out!"

Then he let me have it, like a shot to the brain, "Cause Joyce Lynn Carter died a month ago in Phoenix. Steve, she was a beautiful person but she died of AIDS!"

It was like having a building crumble inside of you, like when we were kids and made those card houses, then someone slammed the door or ran by and it was all suddenly flat on the floor. Poof...and gone! I want to tell you, there is no way to hear this and not feel the crack of the earth under you. It's an awful feeling, and I understand now when I meet people who move back from the quaking fault line of the West Coast to the flat interior. Terror swelled inside of me.

Then Mark told me that he knew from watching all the color drain from my face. It was as though the blood inside me revolted at the news of its own contamination. It was Mark who went to the clinic with me that day and when I got the report from the blood work. It was he who watched me quake. The news was simple and hard as stone. I was *HIV Positive*. My future suddenly had a lid on it, and on that lid was a hard heavy rock marked *AIDS*.

I'll tell you exactly what I did. I threw some food in a backpack, hitched way out of town and began climbing Long Peak, one of the highest points in the Rockys. I told no one, cause I didn't know if I'd be back. I'm sure now that they thought I'd either kill myself or beat it back home to Toledo. But no, I just climbed and climbed in the hard rock of those mountains into the clear cool air where the only pollution was inside of me.

At Longhorn I abandoned the regular trail for one I found off a logging road. There was a riprap of stones half buried along the trail, to hold the hillside and maybe to guide me. Soon I was into the mountain snow and I hadn't even brought a coat. I was ending it, I know now.

For a long time I sat on the rocky edge of a cliff and cried out to the approaching night. I was as hard and cold as the rock ledge and I remember how I just couldn't breathe. It was all an emptiness, you know. Some questions you have to ask even when you know they can't be answered. You just do. But I'll tell you one thing that surprised me was I never really blamed Joy, after that one cry, cause even though she'd given me the death kiss, I was where she was then and I knew the awful aloneness, the need for someone to hold onto.

I cried and I laughed and I sat and I prayed. And I waited. I began to meditate, saying the word "Mu"—nothingness—over and over till it wasn't a word anymore, it was me. I began to drift in and out sitting there but I was awake. And then finally I felt the cool wet grass at my fingers, the hard and steady rocks beneath me. My breath was the wind. It's impossible to say it here, but if you ever get there, you'll know. For a while then I just looked at the blue sky and the brown hills—the sky was the sky, the hills were hills, each one separate and yet both together. They just *were* that's all, they just were.

When I got up and started walking I was cold and dirty, ragged and worn. I came out of the ridge of pines onto a mountain meadow. Across the way I could see in the dusky light a wooden shed of some kind, but by the time I got there it was already night. I climbed inside the old fire shed and lay on the boards that covered some tools. And I'll tell you what

I kept saying to myself were these woodsy lines from a
Snyder poem:
> Lay down these words
> Before your mind like rocks
> placed solid, by hands
> In choice of place. Set
> Before the body of the mind
> in space and time:
> Solidity of bark, leaf, or wall
> riprap of things...

I didn't feel the cold, see, because I was part of it. It was just
all there—it—me—life—all this one thing—and there was no
denying any of it. We're bound together to the end. Sounds
corny but it's true. I knew then that I had to come out to
Boulder to escape myself only to find myself. Even if I can't
say it, it was a feeling like I knew that now and for always my
self included those concrete and solid things placed in space
and time "Before the body of the mind." The boards pressed
into my back and I knew that until I was dead I was real, alive
within the change, and death was maybe just a part of
another change. I could wake and go back to Boulder, all the
way back here to Toledo tonight if needed.

I can't say I don't wake up scared at night scared with
knowing, feeling there's a time bomb inside me, or that I
don't stop and cry watching our sweet human faces on the
bus sometimes. I know I carry around my own destruction,
but we all do, really. I just realize mine in everything. I'm
dying and I'm alive. You know what I'm saying? We're all
dying and we're all alive.

Why am I telling you all this? To scare you about AIDS, I guess, because it is real and has to be reckoned with. But I know it's got to be deeper than that to make me spend my days doing this instead of climbing mountains. Mark said once, maybe I'm reclaiming those last lost years for old Jack. I don't know about that, but I do know I climbed off that mountain because I had to. And all I hope is to somehow help you awaken to what it is we are, to what we have inside, and what we're all a part of.

Now, give me a cup of that coffee, please, and who has the first question?

CLIMBING THE MOUNTAIN

The long trip across the Alleghenies clung to him in the steady thump and roll inside his body as the car paced off the miles. In the high quiet air, he began to sense how the engine's heart faltered slightly, like a murmur, then recovered as it shifted down the hills. You noticed things alone.

To pass the time, he had begun to memorize poems, say them over in his head then out loud to himself as road litanies between sips of coffee or while drinking in the pure landscape of trees and sky. It all came to the same thing, the rhythm of the land and sky, the rhyme of head and heart inside the moment here. Family and job faded with the radio stations in the thin mountain air.

When he first stopped for gas near Clearfield, he waited a moment at his car for the road vibrations to all away, then he stretched his legs and back, press his palms forward against the car's blue roof and leaned into its weight. Mindless, he began gently rocking the car, yet stopped when he saw the young man watching from beside the gas pumps. "What'll it be?"

"Fill her up." Beyond the poems he had been reciting and his own internal talking, these were his first words in hours. "With regular," he added. The T-shirted kid looked up at this crazy man driving a 1970 Volkswagen beetle over these hills alone, even if it was the interstate. The kid shrugged to himself and his long hair shook like leaves in the sharp fall sun. Steven watched its shining about his collar as the boy stood in that motionless stance of youth.

It's all right...he thought...all of it...and it's all just part of this moment. "Well, here we both are," he said to the boy, handing him a ten and asking him to pull it out of the way when he was done.

Steven hopped the step, pushed through the glass doors, and strode into one of those snack bar-service stations. He rested inside the sounds, the steady hum and rumble of dishes and talk. As he approached a seat, each face turned to him blankly from plates of country burgers, turkey hot plate, two eggs sunnyside up. He smiled and melted through them like butter.

The cream paneled restroom at the back offered a sink to splash cold water, a broken commode, and a single urinal where he found himself waiting, while the words of a Wendell Berry poem rolled through his head, "My tasks lie in their place/ where I left them, Asleep like cattle." He stared into the forest green of the stranger's back, "Then what is afraid of me comes/ and lives for a while in my sight."

In a flush, the red faced trucker stepped back, his boot crushing the edge of Steven's Reebok walker. "Sorry, buddy," he laughed, his grin broadening into a smile; then he stepped aside, "Your turn at bat."

Steven nodded as we walked up then rocked into the flow of it. His own urine mixing with all these others in the cold swirling water, all of it going down to somewhere—echoings, like the fellow laughing now into the mirror. Everything was a part of everything.

The man was trying to fix himself. "I got wild hair again," he shouted over to Steven. "Damn wind'll do that to you everytime...give you wild hair." Looking like some grinning kid, his thick brown rose up in a nest of tail feathers at his crown.

"I like it," Steven shouted back. "It's part of the road." Then, staring back at this man, he suddenly reached up and rustled his own hair into its own furry wildness.

"God...damn!" laughed the fellow, and they both stood before the mirror like brothers. "You're as crazy as I am." The sound of the zipper was drowned in the echo of laughter. "Had your lunch yet, buddy?" His whole read rocked No. "Well, come on then, 'cause I'm buying for both us wild hairs."

*****

An hour later, strolling out the auto service side of the station, Steven breathed the afternoon heat. It rested on the pavement, on his shoulders, against his eyes. It was all *there* like the people inside, like the stories of Dan-the-man and his eighteen wheeler. He looked out at the bushy horizon and knew he had three hundred miles to go to New York. He refused to judge the day. "There's lots more where this come from," he said, and slid into the familiar vinyl of his VW. Two dollars and his keys lay on the floor.

Dan hooted three times from his silver semi as he rolled around the end of the building. Dan and his wives, Dan and his dogs, Dan and his lives. Steven sped up and passed him at the entrance to the interstate. The stones came spinning up inside his right fenders, but so what, it was a better way of saying goodbye than his handshake and "May your life go well." You had to talk with your actions on the road.

Steven had told Dan more than he'd planned to tell anyone. Hunched over hot platters of roast beef and potatoes, sucking down coffees, he had said the word monastery, the word Zen, the words inner peace. Dan had grinned through his gravy. "You mean you're going off to become a nun or something?"

Dan rocked back at the counter against the plastic cushion of this stool. "I got you, buddy—a roadrest from the highway of life! I do that myself up in Michigan, only with a fishing pole and a case of Bud. Me and my boy, Rick, go up to Traverse City into the hills of Grand Traverse Bay each spring for a week. You can do lots of your meditating right off the end of your fishing pole in that sunny lake, if you know what I'm saying."

"That's it exactly," Steven nodded. "That's exactly it," but as he stared down at the grains of salt on tan formica between them he knew that for him it was that and more, and that maybe the *more* would keep him from ever knowing that inner peace.

In the midst of restaurant clatter, the two men ate together, and a quiet understanding grew between them. "Did you ever look into your cup, Steve? You see all the circles? Rings I mean...starting with the saucer, then the cup rim, then the tea of coffee, and watch the rings that move outward when you tap it like this." They both stared into it.

...Call it an emptiness or a great void, Steven had tried to fill the hollow of his life with work, with an affair that nearly broke his family apart, then with writing that no one could understand or wanted to publish, finally with jogging down wet roads at night. It was there he had begun to find the silence. Now he was trying to recognize and befriend it through a Zen retreat. Reading one morning after Jane and the kids were gone, he came upon the lines, "...form is no other than emptiness,/ emptiness no other than form;/ Form is exactly emptiness, emptiness exactly form." He wanted to erase those words with his eyes. He wanted to spit it back. Yet something broke a strange laughter inside him. He wanted to swallow it down. It became something he said over in his head while driving down leafy Ohio streets to work, while standing in line at Krogers or gazing out the marina window with the last bite of hot lake perch still on his lips. He knew the echo in the words, the taste of their sound, even believed in them somehow yet couldn't really bring them home inside his life.

He had begun to say them with his breathing at morning and evening meditation as he sat on folded legs over the hardwood floor of his office in the sweet incense. Yet each time, he rose this side of knowing; the stress clearly fallen from his back, yet the dull pain still inside his chest. And so the Zen Mountain Retreat grew in his head like a path he had to climb even if its emptiness proved only to be loss. He had to know it, and touch its cotton in order to come up. Finding this phrase in the Buddhist "Heart Sutra" after his father's death from a heart attack which left him facing his own heart disease seemed another echo of life's karma, like the rings inside Dan's bowl of coffee that pleased him now...'no in, no out...just so.'

Dan touched Steven's sleeve, "What you thinkin,' man? I can feel you driftin' right out the door to somewhere." Then suddenly he lay his spoon between them—"Okay, Wild Hair, I'll bet you this here Bowie knife that you're climbing trees somewhere."

Just as the red haired waitress came through the kitchen door, Steven swept the spoon off the counter and into his palm. Then staring back at Dan, he spoke, "What Bowie knife, white man!"

*****

Gliding now towards the crest of the hill, Steven read the road and slipped into fourth gear. He popped one of the orange Mento candies into his mouth and felt its tangy sweetness, Dan's gift to keep him 'on the road.' And when Dan's silver rig passed him going down the hill, he waved to his wild haired, road brother. He found himself wishing they could take the same road,a nd so reached for the road map, grown soft and worn from folding. Now spreading it across his lap, he fingered its blue and red lines. He'd have to catch Dan at the top of the next hill and signal dinner with him in Bloomburg before their roads divided.

It was already three o'clock and he felt himself rolling within the road, inside the thrust of his car. Mounds of white clouds stretched across the blue, like the mounds of hills echoing across the green. All of it was reflected on his windshield, and Steven felt himself move inside it, gliding forward...while sitting still.

As the hours built into an ache in his back, a stiffness in his shoulders, a soreness around his eyes, he felt his happiness sink into the shadows of the car, the way life seemed to forever fade into black.

*****

When they both pulled off at Bloomsburg, Dan hollered, "Follow me. I know the place to eat." His silver rig like house roared past as it rolled down the hill onto Route 44. A green and white "Bloomsburg—5" reflected in the evening sun. The relief of country roads welcomed them, trading trees and cars for houses and cows as they wound down towards town. "Forty years have I wandered," Steven quoted to himself, "Going east and west." He swung left behind Dan, "Yet returning home I see/ I haven't gone an inch."

Just before Route 11 met 42, they hauled off the road into a gravel parking lot at the crest of a hill. The long building made to resemble a dining car welcomed them with a glow of warm lights in the windows...Mama Dee's Diner—Food and Fuel. Two lone gas pumps stood sentinel at the end of the driveway near a cement block room pained white—Fuel.

Steven watched as Dan walked over to his car, a lighted figure in the setting sun. Dan stretched fully in the golden light, his arms reaching up like branches till suddenly he spun around, "Woo...ee!" he burst and pounded on the roof of the blue beetle. "God, it's good to be alive."

Steven stood in the gravel parking lot stomping his legs back to life. Held by the tiredness he felt Dan slap his shoulder "Well, Steve, can't you feel it—the evening's rest, the food's comfort?" His big hand felt light on Steven's arm."I'll tell you why I love the road...a thousand towns, a million houses, and the road brings you here, just like the moon comes rising in the windows and the pink light rides along the edge of sky." He wrapped his arm around Steven's stooped shoulder as they headed through the clear glass door.

"I thought I lost you there in Milton, buddy, afraid you'd headed off on 180." They strolled past the backs of six men at the counter, smiled at the waitress and a family of four by the door. They found a corner booth, the coolness of leather seats. The waitress poured coffee as she handed them menus, just run off today and shining up through plastic. "Everything's our special, fellows," she smiled. "Right, Dan?" then turned and walked away.

Steven stared at the words, as if some meaning lay there.

"What's the trouble, Steve? You missing home or something?"

He looked over at Dan. They'd only met five hours ago, yet he read him so well. "Sure...that, and other ghosts."

They each sipped their ice water.

Dan nodded to the two kids by the jukebox. "Other families can make you lonesome on the road...I know. But I tell you what I tell myself—you got to recognize what is and isn't there. Beat them ghosts back into the closet with a stare." And Steven noticed for the first time the line of a scar above Dan's eyebrow where the hair hung over. It was more than another line in a face mapped by deep creases.

"You know, you're right," and he drank a deep gulp of ice water. "See, I guess I'm also spooked by this Zen thing. What the hell am I doing anyway? I ought to be home cutting the lawn or painting the garage." Dan just sat there looking back, as somewhere music started playing. "Hell, Wild Man, I'm afraid of everything—afraid I'm being stupid or crazy trying this, afraid I'm an fool if I don't, and I guess afraid I won't measure up." Steven rose into the nostalgic whine of Willie Nelson's "Blue Skies." "Get me the spaghetti with meatballs will you, and a glass of their red wine." He gazed down at Dan who smiled up; then left Dan with the new emptiness of his seat.

The bathroom was close but clean, and Steven washed his hands and face slowly before the mirror staring till he began to to recognize himself.

Returning to his table, Steven noticed a few more faces around the counter, the family gone now, Dan talking to the waitress. "Get your hand off my ass, Dan, or I'll dump this cup of coffee in your lap." And she pulled herself slowly away, smiling as her hair fell softly across her eyes.

Dan laughed loudly, then smiled to Steven, "Caught me rustling, partner. And she done thrown me in the mud." He read the crooked line on Steven's face. "Hey, man we're just kidding around, you dig it, making each other home on the road."

"Yeah, and I suppose you also tickle yourself for laughs."

Dan's eyes rejected this stray comment.

Before them lay their bread and salads, so the two turned to feeding their hunger.

"They make the best Roman bread here...got some kind of cheese and spices on top...it's really fine." And he held out the bread basket, "Here, dip a piece into the wine vinegar on your salad...Man, it's meal enough."

Steven took a bite, felt the juices of his mouth rise to the occasion of the seasoning, watched Dan put himself into his food—elbows extended as he crunched another piece of bread. "Eat when you eat," Steven said.

Dan looked up and toasted his wine glass, "And drink when you drink, buddy."

"Rest when you rest," Steven smiled back, then turned aside, seemed to swallow, made a small sound in the noisy room.

"And burp when you burp, huh?" They both laughed together. Dan spoke with a mouthful, "Let her go, buddy...better out than in."

The last sunlight soon faded from their table,till the only glow was from inside. Amidst the slapping of spaghetti, the crunch of teeth through bread, the sweet taste of wine and hot coffee, they fed on fullness. How was it he felt so at home with this bear of a man? What did either of them know each other? How much did anyone need to know?

When Rose came around with a second cup of coffee, Steven heard himself ask, "Dan, are you going to give me your address so we wild hairs can get together some sweet day?"

He noticed Rose look across at Dan. Then there was a long silent sentence, followed by the period of Dan's "Nope."

Dan watched Steven's face tighten. "Don't you see, man, we don't need it? You can ruin a thing by hanging onto it." Tammy Wynette began a sad country ballad, and Steven looked down into the confusion of his plate. "Besides," added Dan, "we already give each other more than most friends do in a lifetime."

He felt it too. Steven tried not to say anything more, but his heart rose inside his voice, "Dan, I know what you're saying. I do. But are you sure you know what you're doing?"

"Yep...matter of fact, I do." Then, looking across into Steven's hurt eyes, "Now, listen up, man, 'cause I'm telling you your life, here." The two men leaned forward before the dark mirror of the window.

"Steve, seems like you been hurt enough already, and now you gone and started hurting yourself. Just like you're too full right now of Rose's spaghetti and meatballs, but you're still running on empty inside. You're the coffee cup you can't fill 'cause it's already too full of cold coffee and you don't know how to drink it."

Steven pulled back and looked out at the night window and himself.

"Listen, I'll tell you a story." Dan leaned towards Steven's face, "Just listen, will you? Once I hit a deer not very far from here. It was during a bad time in my life when my first wife was leaving me. It was just about this time of night, and I seen it quick but couldn't stop till I did. Then I jumped out and seen her lying there, a doe down in the center of the road. So I grabbed a leg and I pulled her off onto the road berm. She was dead weight, only one thing—she wasn't dead. Anyway, I got her across and she just lay there breathing and staring into me and the night sky."

Steven watched Dan's hands spread before him. "I'm a fisherman, see, but I ain't never hunted in my life. And I never seen a big animal dying at my feet, nor want to again. Well, the deer knew it was dying but it let me touch its soft smooth fur. And I did, I sat there patting it, but knowing all that time that it wasn't no good. Now, Steve, all I could think then was how I wanted to hold onto that deer, to keep it alive somehow, and I was stuck inside my need, see, when what we both needed was a way of letting her go. So I started searching around for something that would show me how. Only all I come up with was a kind of nothing, a rock near the guardrail. And then I seen that this nothing of a rock was the one thing I needed to put this doe out of her misery, and I done it. I just done it before I could think about it. Just done what I had to do. And there it lay all quiet and still as the life went out of it into the air or the night, or me, I don't know. So I just stood there and I felt clean and clear about everything, and I mean everything, man. Including, I took the deer down to the state patrol, and they said they'd take and give her to the county orphanage...least that's what they said."

He was rubbing Steve's arm now, "Anyway, friend, I learned some things that night...and I just hope you can see some of what I'm saying."

And, though the room was still full of noise, still held the sounds of men hungry for food and company, these two sat in a warm pool of silence. For almost five minutes, no one talked. They ate the food on their plates, drank the warm coffee in their cups, and felt each other's quiet.

When Rose came with the check, she spoke softly, "I thought you two had skipped out on me. What's keeping you so quiet—you have a fight or something?"

"No, Rosey. We just talked ourselves out today, and just enjoyed ourselves sucking down your sweet noodles and coffee." Dan was standing then, so he leaned over and kissed her hair softly. "Steve, this here's my first wife, Rose." Nodding to Steve, "Rose, Steve here's on his way to the Adirondacks."

The three stood together, a ring in the warm light at table's end. The music was a softness between them, then rose squeezed Dan's arm and turned to her counter. The two men walked together through the glass door.

There in late dusk, standing above the valley with its web of interweaving roads, the two took each other's hands and shook once. The leaves rustled with new wind, the evening had come and rested in their arms.

"Steve, do you think the rocks pay any attention to the trees?"

"Well, Wild Hair, what are you getting at now?"

"I don't know. I was just noticing today as we passed a lumber truck up around the top of the mountain where the rocks shot out. Seemed the life of a tree ain't much if you're a rock looking at it. What do you think?"

Steven just shook his head for a moment in the night air. Then Dan opened the blue door, and Steven climbed in. "I'll be heading on, wild man."

"You got it, wild man...and don't forget, buddy...to live while you live."

"Yeah," called Steven, "And to...die when you die," as the slag rattled wildly inside the blue fender.

ABOUT THE AUTHOR

Larry Smith is a native of the industrial Ohio Valley, nestled along the Ohio River, within the green walls of the Appalachians. Born and raised in the village of Mingo Junction, Ohio, he grew up in a close family of railroaders and riggers. Amidst the roar of Wheeling-Pitt Steelmills, he worked as a newsboy, playground instructor, delivery person, short order cook, and blast furnace laborer at Weirton Steel. He graduated from Muskingum College and Kent State Univeristy to a career as a teacher, first at Euclid High School, then at Firelands College of Bowling Green State University. He is the director of The Firelands Writing Center and of Bottom Dog Press.

His poetry, fiction, reviews, and personal essays have appeared in a variety of regional and national publications. His literary biographies include: *Kenneth Patchen* (Twayne, 1978) and *Lawrence Ferlinghetti: Poet-at-Large* (1982). He also wrote, and co-produced with Tom Koba, two viodeo programs, *James Wright's Ohio* and *Kenneth Patchen: An Art of Engagement*. In 1980 he and his family lived in Sicily on a Fulbright Lectureship where he lectured on American Romanticism and the Beat Movement.

Poet Richard Hague has written of Smith's *Steel Valley: Postcards and Letters: Poems* (Pig Iron Press, 1992): "He lets us overhear the private griefs and joys...in what becomes a chorus of working class America. Smith stands on back stoops and front porches reading over the shoulders of folk caught up in the paradoxes of Amercans 'so lost and at home with the lives.' "